Judgement of Death

Also by Bob Biderman
The Genesis Files

Judgement of Death

Bob Biderman

Walker and Company
New York

First published in the United States of America in 1992
by Walker Publishing Company, Inc.

Published simultaneously in Canada by Thomas Allen & Son
Canada, Limited, Markham, Ontario

Library of Congress Cataloging-in-Publication Data
Biderman, Bob, 1940-
Judgement of death / Bob Biderman.
p. cm.
ISBN 0-8027-3217-8
I. Title.
PS3552.I335J8   1992   92-4227
813'.54--dc20   CIP

Printed in the United States of America
2 4 6 8 10 9 7 5 3 1

To
Fannie Biderman
A woman of courage

Chapter 1

The sky had a heavy grayness that seemed to swallow all the light. It was as if someone had stuck a pole into a rain-cloud and given it a stir, dispersing the gloom like a blotch of ink dropped in a puddle of water. Joseph took a bite of his sausage-roll and felt the grease run down his chin. It was that sort of day.

He reached inside his pocket, took out a paper towel copped from British Air and used it to wipe his chin. He was sitting on a park bench not too far from the Grand Old Duke of York (the one who had ten thousand men). The Duke was perched some fifty feet up a concrete pole and both of them — he and the Duke, that is — were staring out at a strange assortment of winged rodents fighting over the remains of a cornetto some swastika'd skinhead had tossed in the pond with the panache of a Vandal after the sacking of Rome.

Glancing at his watch, he saw the second hand relentlessly work its way around the dial. It was ten past two. At a quarter of one his plane had landed at Heathrow. Now he was here in a park he had come to ten years before to eat another sausage-roll bought at the same bloody café. Ten years ago it had tasted like crap. This time it tasted worse. It served him right for being a creature of habit, he thought. He looked at the limp and oily thing in his hand and felt his stomach grow sour. Maybe the cook had died. Maybe this was all that was left of him. He gave the thing a heave and watched it plonk into the murky lake below.

Across the avenue that ran ribbon-straight from the Empire's triumphal arch to the palace of the Queen, and set underneath the concrete stairs that led up to the Duke's lookout

7

post, stood the Institute of Contemporary Arts. Surrounded by all the pomp and circumstance, this den of *nouveau* culture seemed to blend into the clubby atmosphere like a chameleon on a desert rock.

A pair of innocuous wooden doors provided an entrance through the imperial wall of stone. Joseph walked inside. Much to his surprise, he suddenly found that he felt quite at home. One of Darwin's little discoveries that eventually shook the world was the relationship between protective coloration and survival. From the inside, all international sanctuaries for artists had much the same look of defiance, whether they were in New York, London, Paris or Rome; but they still had to blend into a hostile world, he supposed.

It didn't take him long; he recognized her at once. She was standing in the alcove that passed for a trendy bookshop, glancing through a miniature volume of Masereel woodcuts. He came up behind her.

"You ever see anything by Rockwell Kent?" he said. "Amazing what stories those guys could tell with just a chisel and a block of wood."

She turned and gave him a quick once-over with her enormous eyes. "Are you an authority on chisels?" she asked. "Or do you just like talking to yourself out loud?"

He looked half-apologetic. "You're not Kate O'Malley?" he asked. "Short brown hair, five foot two, a little heavy on the eye makeup . . . you really do fit her description."

She raised her eyebrows. "Joseph Radkin? Tall, dark and handsome?" She shook her head. "You don't."

He smiled and stuck out his hand. "Pleased to meet you, Kate."

"I'd hold off deciding if you're pleased or not until we've had a chance to speak," she said as she gave his hand a shake. "Coffee?"

"Why not?" He gave a quick look around. "Where?"

She jerked her thumb toward a hallway on the other side of the room. "There."

He followed her across and watched her flash a card at a

bored attendant sitting with his feet up on a table, reading a punky fashion magazine.

"What did you show him?" asked Joseph. "Your artist's license?"

"It costs sixty pence to get in if you're not a member," she explained as she moved swiftly down the hall, ignoring the walls and what passed for an exhibit.

Joseph took a quick look at the canvases on display. "They should pay us," he said.

"Try Piccadilly, if you like your nudes on velvet, chum," she replied without giving him a second glance.

The hallway led into a large, multilevel space. The balcony had a bar, very chicly black on white, a huge mirror to admire yourself in or cause yourself to cringe, and windows that looked out onto the promenade. The lower level had a series of café booths with smooth, flowing lines that turned themselves into curlicues the 1930s took for style. To the left and through an arch, you could see a self-service arrangement of salads and stuff sitting prettily behind some glass just like it would have been in California. If you had a nose for curry you might have smelled it back there too.

"Nice," he said. "Very art deco . . ."

"Glad you approve," she replied. "Are you having anything to eat? You are on an expense account, aren't you?"

He shook his head. "Not yet. I'm still negotiating though."

She sighed. "If we're only having coffee, it's better at the bar. They have an espresso machine."

"A woman after my own heart." Joseph winked.

She made a grimace. "All you Yanks have the same line, don't you?"

"Depends on where we're coming from," he said, following her up the balcony stairs.

"It seems to me you're all coming from New York or California."

"The ones who say they come from California really came from New York first," said Joseph. "But I meant in their head."

9

"Then they're not coming very far." She glanced at the barman. "Two coffees, please."

The barman pointed to the clock on the wall and said, "Sorry. The bar closes at half-two."

Kate looked back at Joseph and shrugged. "Too late."

"For what?" he asked. "I know the English make drunkenness obligatory by forcing everyone to drink by the clock, but I didn't realize you did that with coffee, too!"

"The machine's behind the bar," said the attendant, taking a cloth and wiping a few sudsy glasses without bothering to give them a rinse.

"He's American," Kate explained.

"I know," said the barman. "You can tell them a mile away."

"Is it a disease?" asked Joseph. "Do I have spots?"

"You might say that," said Kate.

"This no-coffee thing is a joke, right?" Joesph looked at her, expecting a chuckle.

She shook her head. "I'm afraid not."

Joseph turned to the barman. "How about just giving us some coffee, pal? You're standing there, we're standing here. All it takes is for you to press that button." He pointed to the switch on the machine.

"Sorry," said the barman.

"Why are you sorry?" Joseph went on. "Are you sorry that you can't make us a cup of coffee? Because if you are there's an easy way to make amends . . ."

The barman looked him in the eye. "I was going to say I was sorry I let the steam out of the machine," he said in reply. "But actually, I'm not."

"Why didn't he just tell us that he let the steam out of the machine to begin with?" Joseph asked. They were sitting in one of the booths drinking coffee from the café below. He made a face. "What do you think they used to make this stuff? Dishwater?"

"The English are more circumspect than you Americans. They have trouble saying things straight out."

10

He looked at her. "What do you mean, 'the English'? What are you?"

"Irish."

"Historically, you mean. You sure sound English to me."

"'Sounding' and 'being' are two different things."

"I didn't hear you put up much of a fight about the espresso."

"You become stoic if you live here long enough." She hesitated a moment and then said, "Mike had difficulty with that, too . . ."

"I imagine," said Joseph putting more sugar in his cup. "I never drink coffee with sugar," he explained, "but this stuff . . ."

"Don't suffer over it," she said. "Get yourself some tea."

"Tea?" He gave her a pained look. "Is that what it'll come to if I end up staying here?"

She put down her cup and stared at him. "Are you going to end up staying here?"

"I don't know." He gave his coffee another stir. "Tell me about Mike."

"What did your big chief tell you?"

He shrugged. "Just that he had an accident. Run over while he was walking down a country road. Something like that."

She took out a cigarette and lit up. "Perhaps . . ."

He stared at her a moment. "'Perhaps'?" Then, pointing to her pack, he said, "Let me have one of those."

"I thought all Americans were afraid of getting cancer," she said, sliding the pack his way.

"Well, was he run over or not?" asked Joseph, taking one of her smokes and leaning forward as she lit up a match.

"Yes, he was run over. But perhaps it wasn't an accident."

He looked at her through a cloud of smoke. "Are you trying to tell me that he committed suicide by throwing himself in front of a truck?"

"Mike wasn't suicidal. What do you know about the story he was working on?" she asked him.

"Just general stuff . . . West told me you had the files."

11

"West!" She made a face of intense dislike. "He's a prat!"

"You know him?"

"I met him once. He flew in for the weekend. You Americans do things like that, don't you?"

"Only the wealthy ones. The rest of us scratch for a living like everyone else. You didn't like our lovable leader, huh?"

"I've met his type before. Glib, charming, offer you the moon and give you moldy cheese." She stubbed out her cigarette.

"He's not so bad," said Joseph. "I've met a lot worse. He's still got a few principles."

She let out an icy laugh. "Principles? Is that what you call them?"

"Listen, lady," he said with some annoyance, "I come from a place where most people eat scruples for breakfast and shit 'em out for tea. In this business nobody's clean."

"Well that's America in a nutshell, I guess," she said with a smirk.

"Who the hell are you to talk? You guys still got a queen!"

Her eyes were flashing like angry stop signs. "I told you before, I'm Irish!"

"And I've got an uncle who once lived in Timbuktu!" he shot back. "What's that supposed to mean?"

She sighed. "Listen, Radkin, I didn't meet you here to argue the relative depths we've sunk to in our trade."

"Why did you meet me then?"

She suddenly seemed different to him now. There was a more compassionate look in her eyes as she said, "I wanted to give you fair warning. There's only trouble here. Why don't you just go back where you belong."

Chapter 2

They were standing on the pavement just outside the ICA. The wetness seeped from the stone and hung in the air like the remnants of a tropical rain mixed with a bit of arctic frost. Joseph took off his glasses and wiped them on his shirt. "You ever dry out in this country?" he asked.

"Only between three and six," she said looking at him and narrowing her eyes. "It's up to you, Radkin. If you want I'll take you to my place and give you Mike's files. But if I were you, I'd take the other half of your ticket and fly back to San Francisco today."

"My ticket's only one-way." He tossed her a grin.

She shrugged. "Suit yourself, Rambo." Then she waved at a taxi speeding down the other side of the avenue.

"Hey! What's wrong with the subway?" he asked, as a black Austin performed a neat U-turn and dieseled to the curb.

"You mean the underground? There's no tube station where we have to go," she said, opening the taxi door. "Besides, you must have a travel allowance." She gave him a significant look. "Don't you?"

He made a face and followed her into the cab. Kate leaned toward the front and told the driver: "Gospel Oak. Rona Road. You know it?"

The cabby nodded and started off.

"Rona Road?" said Joseph. "I thought that's where Mike lived . . ."

"Yeah. Across the street."

Joseph settled back in his seat and then wiped his hand over the side window to clear his view. He pressed his nose against the glass as they sped past the park. "I met an old dame there a

13

while ago — one of your tweedy types. She told me something really weird."

Kate was straightening her hair as she turned to him. "What?"

"It was about this guy who stopped to feed the birds . . ."

"People sometimes do that here, Radkin. It's one of our quainter customs . . ."

"Yeah, well he fed them something that put a little crimp in their style."

"Poison?"

Joseph nodded.

"I suppose it just goes to show that America doesn't have a patent out on loonies . . ."

"She said he looked very respectable. She called him a gentleman."

"The upper class here delights in killing things that fly," said Kate. "You ought to spend a day out on the moors."

"They don't usually do it in parks, I bet."

"Maybe he was just overanxious."

"I thought the idea was to give them a sporting chance," said Joseph.

"You've never been on a fox-hunt, I assume . . ."

"No, I prefer a good film." He shot her a questioning glance and caught her eye. "Have you?"

"I did a story on the anti-hunt movement once . . ."

"And?"

She made a face of intense dislike. "They're a pretty bloodthirsty mob!"

"The anti-hunt movement?"

"The fox-hunters!" ·

"Well, maybe that's how Britain was able to rule the world."

"By hunting fox?"

"By being bloodthirsty."

"What's your excuse?" she asked.

He looked at her innocently. "Us? We just want to make the world safe for democracy."

"Sure."

He laughed. "OK. So sarcasm isn't your strong card. How did you meet Mike?"

"By being sarcastic. He said he liked my eyes. I told him I had a pair of lovely knuckledusters, as well."

"That's not sarcasm," said Joseph. "That's straight out hostility."

She shrugged. "Take it any way you like."

"What paper do you work for again? The *Blood and Guts Gazette*?"

"*Cityscapes*. It's an entertainment magazine. I'm doing a feature article on prisons for them."

"About body-racks and thumb-screws? Things like that?"

She glared at him. "Well what the hell is that rag you work for? The only thing you're missing is the picture on the cover of a lurking maniac holding a dripping knife and a naked woman screaming to be raped."

"*Investigations* isn't that bad!" he said defensively.

"Not quite!"

"It started out as a good idea . . ."

"So did sex."

"You got something against sex?" he asked.

"I have a six-year-old kid, a two-year-old mortgage and fifty quid in the bank. I think I've been screwed enough, thank you."

"How about Mike?"

"Mike was just something on the side."

He nodded. "I see."

"No you don't!" she said, throwing him a nasty look.

"I've got a wife and a couple of kids of my own," he admitted.

"Where are they? You ditch 'em?" she asked.

"Ditch 'em? You've been watching too many American gangster films."

"Any American film is a gangster film — made by gangsters about gangsters for gangsters."

"You've got a real sweet vision of the land of the free

15

and the home of the brave. But for your information, I didn't run out on them, if that's what you mean. Polly might come over after I've settled in and found a place . . ."

"Polly — is that your wife or your parrot?"

"She's whatever she wants to be when she wants to be it."

"Sounds good to me."

"I thought it would."

Maybe it was his admission, but her demeanor changed. She seemed less harsh. "How did you get involved with West?" she asked.

"I knew him from university. We worked on the school magazine together," Joseph said. "After that we lost touch. I bumped into him one day in San Francisco. He heard I'd been canned . . ."

"'Canned?' What's that? Pickled or tinned?"

"Gotten the sack, made redundant . . ."

"Screw the boss's wife? Steal the take? Come on, Radkin, what lovely thing did you do to get the sack?"

"I wrote a story that blew the whistle on the wrong sort of people. My publisher got hit with a libel suit he wouldn't defend."

"Doesn't sound like the best of references, Radkin. Even for someone like West."

"I told you," said Joseph, "he's not that bad . . ."

"He's not that good, either."

"He's done some damn good things, if you really want to know. The idea of *Investigations Magazine* is fantastic . . ."

"'Fantastic' is probably the right word. What was the idea behind it anyway?"

"Taking some old cases that really stirred people up fifty or a hundred years ago and reopening them again . . ."

"Yeah, I know all that — but what's the great idea?"

"The idea is making the contemporary link. Like with the Maybrick case. Here's an American woman who marries a British cotton merchant and gets convicted of poisoning him

16

with arsenic — which businessmen in those days used to get high. A hundred years later, a woman is convicted of poisoning her hotshot lover with cocaine. In both cases the men were known users — but of the upper-class, respectable sort. The women were accused of tampering with the dose. That has the seeds of a great story, doesn't it?"

"If you force it enough it might."

"It sure as hell does! Besides, after a hundred years the records are opened up to the public. That's why West was so insistent on getting an ace journalist like me to follow it up after Mike . . . resigned."

She looked at him incredulously while her jaw dropped an inch. "'Resigned'? Is that what you Yanks call it? I suppose you call a monkey's ass 'bananas'?"

"No, we call it a 'tush'. How far into the story did he get?"

"I don't know. I think he got sidetracked."

"Sidetracked? What do you mean?"

"He kept good notes. Everything's there for you to see, Radkin. I didn't eat any of it, I promise!"

"Why did he keep his files at your place, Kate?"

"He didn't. Unfortunately he spent a good deal of time in my bedroom, so I became his answering service — at least, that's what West seemed to think. When Mike . . . resigned . . . West asked me to pick up the records and hold them for you. He was afraid that otherwise they'd have been confiscated by the police."

"Thanks."

"I didn't love him," she said, turning away and looking out her window, "but he was a decent sort . . . unlike a lot of men I know. I wouldn't mind finding out what happened to him myself."

He looked over at her. She had a frailness of appearance that was about a hundred and eighty degrees windward of the words that came out of her mouth. "What makes you so certain Mike was bumped off?"

She turned back and met his eye. He saw something in them

17

he didn't expect. "Nothing but my gut," she said as casual as you please.

"Do you consider yourself a journalist or a reporter?" he asked her.

"Is this an American language quiz?" she replied. "What do I win if I guess right? A trip to Disneyland?"

He smiled. "In my book, Kate, there are journalists and reporters. Reporters cite facts. For journalists, instinct means a lot."

She made a show of taking a notebook from her purse. "You mind if I write that down?"

"Write whatever you damn well like . . ."

She put her hand over her mouth. "Oh . . . have I hurt your itsy bitsy feelings? Would an apology to your Embassy suffice? 'So sorry to have squandered advice from card-carrying American . . .'"

"Go stuff yourself!" he muttered, turning away.

"What a pompous ass!" She crossed her arms and looked straight ahead. Outside, rows of desolate housing appeared like a running collage of post-depression squalor.

There was a minute of silence, then he said, "Look, I don't know what you got against Americans, but . . ."

She turned back to him. There was fire in her eyes: "How do I hate thee? Let me count the ways . . ." And she began ticking off the list on her fingers. "Cruise missiles, Yuppies, Ford, Grenada, the Lybian bombing, Kentucky Fried Chicken, McDonalds . . ."

He held up his hand. "Whoa there, sister! You're not gonna blame me for fast-food chains. Anyway, what about Wimpies?"

". . . Vietnam . . ."

"That was fifteen years ago! If you're going back that far I can start listing things too: Suez, Malaysia . . ."

"The CIA!"

"MI5!"

"Nicaragua!"

"Ireland!"

18

They glared at each other like swordless gladiators on a marshy field of battle. And then, suddenly, they both began laughing.

"You're a jerk," she said, catching her breath as if feeling herself go soft.

"OK," he replied. "So I'm a jerk and you're a bigot. Why should that stop us from being friends?"

"That's the problem with you Yanks," she said, "you offer friendship with one hand while you're picking a pocket with the other."

"It didn't seem to stop you being friends with Mike Rose," he reminded her.

"Mike Rose was different."

"Most of us are."

She closed her eyes and sighed. "Listen, Radkin. It's been a difficult fortnight. Sean really misses him . . ."

"Sean?"

"My little boy. He and Mike hit it off." She made a face. "Mike taught him to play baseball."

"It's better than drugs," Joseph replied.

"Yeah. OK. I'm . . . sorry."

"Journalists don't apologize," he said.

"Fuck you!"

"I thought you were tough."

"You don't know how tough I am!"

He nodded. "I guess we'll get along all right," he said as the taxi pulled over to the side of the road.

Chapter 3

She had the bottom flat of a red-brick, terraced job that looked out on a pretty, tree-lined street. There was a front garden that was cluttered up with kiddy toys and rubbish that might have been hauled away if one only had the time.

"Who lives upstairs?" asked Joseph as they walked up to the door.

"A couple. He's an artist. She's a social worker. They babysit for me sometimes."

"Makes life a little easier, I guess," Joseph said.

"Besides a fatter paycheck, the only thing right now that might make life a little easier is the assurance that we won't all get blown up tomorrow night," Kate replied, reaching into her purse and getting out the key.

Joseph noticed that her body had suddenly stiffened, like a cat sniffing danger.

"Something wrong?" he asked.

"Yes." He caught the worried look in her eye. "The door . . . it's open."

"Maybe you forgot to lock it," he suggested.

"You think I'm an idiot? I've got a computer in there!" she said, staring at him as if he were mad.

She pushed at the door. It swung open exposing the box-like living room. She walked inside. He followed.

"Seems like someone did a pretty good job of ransacking the place," said Joseph, going over and picking up some books that were scattered on the floor and placing them back in the bookcase.

"I don't know," she said, shaking her head, "it usually looks this way. I don't have much time to straighten up."

"My place isn't exactly right for fancy teas either, if it makes

20

you feel any better." Joseph moved a heap of clothes to one side of a lumpy couch and sat down.

"Why should that make me feel any better?" she said, putting her hands on her slender waist and staring at him.

He shrugged. "I'm sorry if it made you feel worse."

She glared at him a moment longer, without making a reply, and then she left. He could see her through the hallway walking up the stairs. Picking up a book that was still on the floor, he began paging through. A moment later, he heard her coming down again. He put aside the book and watched her come back into the living room. He could tell from her expression that something wasn't right.

"What is it, Kate?"

She looked unsettled and confused. "Mike's files," she said. "They're gone."

Her kitchen looked out onto an overgrown patio and was about the size of a Volkswagen Beetle. There was a wooden table that took up most of the space leaving just enough room for a sink, a doll's house size fridge, a stove which she charmingly called a "cooker", and a beat-up washing-machine. The only other visible accoutrement was a clothes-line strung across the length of the room, on which was hung a few dainty garments like lady's underthings and children's socks.

They were sitting at the table drinking tea. As if that wasn't bad enough, she had offered him some powdered milk to top it up.

"What do you think?" he asked her.

"How the hell should I know?" she said in reply.

Joseph rubbed the bristles on the side of his face as he watched her stick a knife into a gob of warm butter and spread it on some bread. "Who knew Mike's stuff was here, Kate?"

She looked up at him and pointed with her knife still covered in goo. "I'm not a spy, Radkin. I wasn't trying to cover my tracks! I just went across the street and told Mrs White exactly what your lovely editor told me . . ."

"What exactly did West tell you?"

"That Mike had done some research on an article and that you were coming over to take his place and would I mind picking up the files and keeping them for you."

"So it must have been White who blew the whistle . . ."

"What do you mean, 'blew the whistle'? There wasn't any mystery, Radkin! I didn't ask her to sign the Official Secrets Act!" She watched him rub his chin again. "Trying to gauge the length of your designer stubble? How do you guys do it, anyway?"

"Do what?"

"Never look like you have a beard; always look like you need a shave."

He shook his head. "What's Mike's landlady like?"

"She's an elderly woman. Lace-curtain Irish . . ."

"Meaning?"

"She has curtains made of lace!"

"What is it she runs — a Victorian boarding-house?"

"She has an upper flat that she rents out."

"Mike had family who lived in London, didn't he?"

"Yeah. A rich bitch of a mother who lives up on Hampstead hill. She's English. His father was a Yank. When Mike's father died, she moved back and married Cecil Hughes."

"Who's he?"

"A guy who thinks the earth trembles whenever he moves."

"Does it?"

"It probably does."

"You know Mike's mother?"

"I met her once. That's enough."

Joseph looked at the dangling underclothes and pictured the Mike he knew. "You sure couldn't tell he came from money."

"That's what I liked about him," she said.

"That flat across the street, is it furnished?"

"You could say so. It has the basics: a couch, a chair, a desk, a bed . . ."

"How about a telephone?"

"Mike had one installed. I suppose it's still there. Why?"

"You think she'd rent it to me?"

22

Kate let out a sigh. "I thought you might be leading up to that."

"Well?"

She got up from her chair and piled the cups with the other dirty stuff in the sink. "I think she'd be hesitant." Kate turned to face him. "She's a little tired of Americans who bloody up her place."

"You mean there've been others? Anyway, I thought Mike got run over by a truck outside of town."

"I was speaking metaphorically, Radkin."

"What if I promise not to bloody up my metaphors?" he said, casting an eye at the dishes in her sink. "You and White must get on swell!"

"As a matter of fact, we do!" Kate angrily pulled down her laundry.

"Good!" said Joseph with one of his patented smiles. He got up from his chair. "You can introduce me then!"

The house across the street had the scrubbed-down look of a choirboy. Joseph, whose relationship to church was similar to a kid and a castor-oil factory, had a sudden impulse to turn around and run the other way. It was, however, too late to think again. Kate had already pressed the buzzer.

Mrs White was just like her name — her skin and hair had the tone of elderly cream cheese; her eyes were a neutral shade of grey. In striking contrast, however, the outfit she was wearing was black. Joseph thought she wouldn't have looked out of place in the neighbourhood mortuary.

"It's a terrible day," she said, looking up at the sky. "I can never put out the washing!"

"This is Mr Radkin," said Kate. "He was a colleague of Mike's."

The old woman shook her head in the manner of someone who'd just come from a wake. "What a terrible waste! What a sin! For a man so young and not yet properly engaged!" She glanced slyly at Kate who momentarily dropped her eyes.

"Violet," Kate began, looking back up at her again, "Mr Radkin was wondering what plans you had for Mike's room."

Mrs White appeared surprised. "His room? Dear God! I've not yet changed the linen!"

Joseph gazed at her sympathetically. "Michael and I were good friends," he said. "Many's the evening we spent together at the Starry Plough, talking about the old country . . ."

"Are you Irish, Mr Radkin?" she asked.

"In my heart, Mrs White," he said, putting his right hand over his breast. "In my heart." Joseph glanced up at the house. "I was just telling Kate how much this looks like my childhood home . . ." He looked back at Mrs White and tried to open his eyes wide enough to force a little moistness. "Please call me Joseph," he said.

His boyish charm seemed to melt through her suspicious demeanor. "And have you been here long, Joseph," she said, giving him what he interpreted as a quasi-maternal look.

"I just arrived today, Mrs White. Ten hours in the sky without a wink of sleep."

"Then you'd like a drop of tea," she said, "and perhaps a fresh baked scone?" She opened the door a little wider now to let them in.

"A fresh baked scone? My dear Mrs White! How did you know?"

"Know what?" she asked.

"That I've been dreaming of just that! A fresh baked scone!"

A ray of light came to her eyes. A smile came to her lips. "Isn't he a lovely lad?" she said to Kate.

Kate's eyes were rolling in her head. "Yes, he really is full of it, isn't he?" Looking down at her watch, she added, "I've got to pick up Sean now. I'll have to pass on tea." And, as an aside to Joseph, she whispered, "Doesn't seem as if you'll need any help from me."

He winked at her and, with a flourish of professional pride, like a peacock spreading his feathers, he turned and followed Mrs White down the sanitized hallway.

*

24

He allowed her to change the linen but insisted she didn't clean. For his tastes it was overscrubbed already. She showed him how to put coins into the meter box to keep the electricity on and how to light the fire to keep down the chill and the damp. Finally, after an hour of chat that parched his throat as well as his mind, struggling for the medium between banality and wit that seemed to charm people like Mrs White, she left him alone.

Now, as he toured the lifeless rooms on his own, he wondered whether he had done the right thing. He went to the front window, held back the curtains — Kate was right, they were lace — and peeked outside. It all looked so cold and bleak. He let the curtains drop, put his hands in his pockets and sighed.

By the far wall was an enormous wooden desk. On top of the desk was an ancient Underwood upright and a fairly old telephone. He went over to the typewriter and tested out the keys like a musician would have done if left in a room with an antique piano. He sat down in the chair behind the desk, placed his fingers on the keyboard and typed out a tune on the sheet of paper that had already been rolled inside: "Every good boy does fine if given ha-f a chance to jump over the -azy fox . . ." The "l" stuck. Well, he could fix that. He picked up the receiver. The other project of import seemed to work as well. So, he thought, if nothing else he had the tools of his trade. The big double "T": the typewriter and the telephone.

He looked at his watch and tried to figure out what time it was in San Francisco. He had left in the afternoon and had arrived here the morning of the next day. The flight was ten hours long. There was a hunk of time that had evaporated from his life. Where had it gone? Into the sky like watery gases drawn up into the atmosphere, he supposed. Perhaps it would be returned to him if he flew back again. Then he thought, maybe not.

Looking in the phone directory placed neatly by its master, he found the international dialing code for the USA. He placed the call and waited for the ring.

It took a while for her to answer: "Hello?"

"Polly! Hi, it's me."

Her voice sounded groggy. "Oh, Joseph . . . are you OK?"

"Yeah, fine. Why wouldn't I be?"

"I don't know . . . you woke me from a dream."

"Were you asleep? I'm sorry," he apologized. "I should have waited, I guess."

"No. I'm glad you called. I was beginning to worry."

"How are the kids?"

"Tanya's got a cold. Your mother's been watching her while I'm at work."

"How's Abe?"

"He's OK. He painted the back of someone's neck at playgroup. Caused a little stir, not much. How are you? Did you meet your contact yet?"

"Kate O'Malley? Yeah. She's a real gas. Short and tough. You'd love her Pol. She fixed me up with a place to stay."

"Where?"

"Mike's old rooms. Turns out he lived across the street."

"That must be sort of spooky, Joseph. I think it would give me the shudders to move in where someone had just died. Even if it was an accident."

"Kate thinks he was bumped off . . ."

"What?"

He bit his tongue. "Nothing."

"Did you say 'bumped off'?"

"I don't know . . . maybe I did . . . it just sort of slipped out."

"Well, for God's sake, Joseph! Does she think he was bumped off because of the story you're replacing him on?"

"No . . . she said he got sidetracked."

"What the hell does that mean?"

"I don't know."

"Did you know about this when West offered you the job?"

"No."

"Abe and Tanya are way too young to be orphaned, Joseph. Why can't you write your story back home?"

26

He hesitated a moment. Then he said, "All Mike's stuff —
all his research is . . . missing."

"That's a pretty lame excuse!"

"Listen, Polly, I've got to see it out. You know how long
I've been waiting for a chance like this! For the last couple of
years I've been busting my balls doing free-lance work and
hardly earning a dime. Now I've got a chance to work for a
decent wage, doing what I do best — investigative journalism . . ."

"Digging up bones!"

"You're the archeologist, Polly."

"Social anthropologist, damn it! And I don't put my life in
danger doing my job."

"I don't either. I'm good at what I do. I don't take foolish
chances, you know that."

"What about that breaking and entry business."

"When?"

"You know when!"

"Polly, I promise you. I'll be as careful as a mouse . . ."

". . . who got caught in a cheesy trap!"

"Who slyly retreated to his hole when there was any hint of
danger."

There was silence at the other end of the line.

"Polly, are you still there?"

"Yes, I'm still here . . ."

"Well, say something."

Her voice was soft and entreating. "I love you, Joseph.
Please be careful."

"I'll be careful, Polly. I promise."

He heard her sigh again. "Give me the address and
telephone number where you're staying."

He gave her what she wanted and then he hung up.

The only thing he had with him, besides the clothes he was
wearing, was his notebook and his pen. His luggage was
stowed at Victoria Station when he took the train from
Heathrow into town that morning. Sitting at the desk — once

Mike's, now, temporarily, his own — he opened his notebook and glanced through his scrawls. He was probably the only one who could have deciphered them.

The story was as simple as it was complex. A hundred years ago a young American woman, Florence Chandler, was travelling to England. Aboard ship she had met a gentleman, somewhat older than herself — a Liverpool cotton-broker named Maybrick. She was beautiful, he seemed charming. They fell in love. He took her home. It was there in Liverpool that her prince had paled. Florence, though from American wealth, didn't fit into the Liverpool of Queen Victoria's day. She was, as they put it, too full of herself. Not even the servants gave her the loyalty someone in her position might expect. She was a stranger in their midst, an alien. And as the years went on, she began to see herself as a prisoner in her husband's house.

She bore him two children, a son and a daughter. Then, one day, she discovered a dark secret. Somewhere hidden in the depths of Liverpool's slums was another woman with children fathered by her husband. And she discovered something else. She found he had a craving of the most pernicious sort and, as his business neared collapse, this need had grown.

In the depths of her misery, Florence Maybrick met a man, her husband's friend, who offered her solace. They had a brief affair, consummated one weekend in a country hotel. Not too long after that, her husband lay dead. The Maybrick family accused Florence of poisoning him with arsenic.

The subsequent events were followed closely by the press, eager for any new salacious thrill. The headlines were the sort that read: "Beautiful American Heiress Accused of Poisoning Husband after Liaison with Friend!" The crowds came with their picnic lunches, hoping to find a vacant courtroom bench. Women dressed up in their finest frocks. Men had worn their spats. It was the kind of gruesome living theatre that draws the worst from people — and the best. And standing friendless in the dock was the American, Florence Maybrick, née Chandler, accused of murder and on trial for her life. Two days later, the judge had put a piece of black cloth atop his head and sentenced her to death.

Joseph turned the page and took out several contemporary press clippings which had been folded up inside. One was headlined: "Woman Accused of Murdering Aristo Lover with Poisoned Cocaine." The other read: "Lavinia Chancellor Convicted of Murder. Sentenced to Twenty Years in Prison." He read them over and when he was done, folded them neatly, put them back inside his notebook and closed it up again.

Chapter 4

It was dark by the time he made his way back across the street to Kate's place. There was a chill wind that ran through his body like water through a worn-out sieve. Joesph hunched up his shoulders and knocked on the door. After a couple of minutes the door opened up and she stared out at him. Her clothes were plastered with brownish muck. She looked like she had fallen into a cement mixer filled with chocolate pudding. "What do you want now?" she asked.

"Talk?"

"I was feeding my kid."

"Looks like he was feeding you."

"We have a mutual understanding."

"It's cold out here," said Joseph, pulling up the collar of his jacket to cover his neck. "Can I come in?"

A little voice from inside shouted out: "Mummy, who's there?"

She made a face as she opened up the door to allow him inside. "Now I'm going to have to explain you to him."

"Just say I'm the resident Yank," Joseph replied, pulling down his collar again and following her into the kitchen.

A little red-cheeked boy with huge brown eyes, just like his mother's, sat at the table playing with an off-colored bowl of goo. He gave Joseph a quizzical look as he came in.

"Hi, Sean," said Joseph, giving the boy's flaxen hair a ruffle. "How's tricks?"

The boy smiled and pointed at Joseph. "He talks like Mikey!" he said with seemingly enormous delight.

"Now you've done it, haven't you?" said Kate, going over to the sink and filling up the kettle.

"Are you Mikey?" asked the boy, tilting his head as if

30

Joseph might possibly transform into someone else if looked at from another way.

"No, my name's Joseph. I knew your friend, Mikey, though . . ."

"Mikey went away," said the boy.

"I know," said Joseph.

"He's not coming back," said the boy with all the certainty of a six-year-old.

Joseph looked over at Kate who had turned to put the kettle on the stove. He saw her brush away a tear.

"You know, I have a little boy, too," said Joseph turning back to the child.

"How old?" asked the boy, cocking his head again.

"A little younger than you."

"Where is he?"

"In San Francisco. That's a city in the USA."

"I know that," said the boy, wrinkling his nose. "Mikey lived there, too."

"Anyway, I talked to him tonight on the telephone and he told me to give you this . . ." Joseph reached into his pocket and took out a pair of miniature wings.

The boy's eyes lit up as he took the plastic wings in his little hand. "What is it?" he asked.

"It's what the stewardess gives you if you're silly enough to fly with her across the ocean."

"I've never been across the ocean," said the boy, moving the wings through the air in an up and down motion and then crashing them into his pudding.

"All right, Muffin," Kate said, coming over with something weak and brown and setting it before Joseph. She lifted her son out of his chair, "You'll have to save your acrobatics till the morning. Time for your bath."

"What is this stuff?" asked Joseph, looking down at the cup.

"Bovril. I thought you didn't like tea."

"I like Bovril less."

"Well," she said, heading toward the stairs, her boy slung

31

over her arm, "make yourself a Marmite sandwich. Then you won't care what you drink."

He was hungry enough to follow her advice. He found a jar labeled "Marmite" and spread some on a slice of bread. He took a bite and chewed. The taste to him was something between axle grease and homemade shampoo.

"What is that crap you had me eat?" he shouted upstairs after dumping the sandwich in his Bovril cup.

"You mean the Marmite? You don't like that either?"

"Did Mike?"

"Not much. You Yanks don't seem to like anything but hamburgers."

"You got any of them?"

"What?"

"Hamburgers."

"Why don't you try hiking up to Hampstead, Radkin. You'll find plenty of things to like up there . . . that is if you still have something in your wallet."

"How far is it?"

"Not too."

"Want to join me?"

She appeared at the top of the stairs, her hands covered in soap suds and strands of hair pasted to her face. "Does it look like I can join you?" she said.

"Why don't you ask your upstairs neighbors if they'll babysit."

"Are you treating me to dinner, Radkin?"

"Did I say that?"

She shook her head as if to show how much a failed case she thought he was. Then she turned and started to walk away.

"All right," he called out to her. And then in a lower voice he said, "But try to make it someplace not too expensive."

The Dome Café was almost at the top of Hampstead High Street. Almost, but not quite. To get there from Gospel Oak, they had to walk to South End Green, past the pizza joint where Orwell worked when pizzas had been books, and up along the heath and down a road where Keats had strolled some years before. If Keats had eaten at the Dome Café, Kate O'Malley never said.

The place wouldn't have looked bad on a Paris boulevard, though that may have been the point. The glass partitions in the front opened out onto the street giving the appearance of a sidewalk café — even if the lack of pavement made it not the real thing. Inside, the tables were squeezed tight on the periphery giving center stage to the bustling bar. The walls had a thin layer of nicotine permanently embossed. The decor was French Gitanes. The smoke was thick.

"Feel secure?" she asked him.

Joseph glanced around. "Newspapers on racks, a cappuccino machine and bottled beer." He looked at her and smiled. "Hey, are there many places like this around?"

"Just enough for you young upwardly mobiles to meet," she said, picking up the glossy menu. "The rest of us hang out at the neighbourhood caff working our way through sausage and mash."

"How about the middle-aged downwardly drifting folk like me? Where do we go?"

She didn't look up from her menu. "Try the Salvation Army."

They placed their order with the harried waiter.

"Your kid and Mike were pretty close?" he said as the waiter wandered off.

She nodded. "You could say that, I suppose. There aren't a lot of males in his life . . ."

"Father?"

She shrugged.

"Grandparents?"

"Somewhere else."

"You want to tell me about Mike?"

She shook her head. "No."

"Did you call the cops?"

"Why should I have done that?"

"To tell them about the theft! People do that here when they're burgled, don't they?"

"Nothing else is missing except his files. And his files didn't belong to me. Besides, it's probably the police who did it."

"Why would the cops have stolen Mike's files? If they wanted them they could have come and asked. Am I right?"

She stared at him without speaking.

"There's something else that puzzles me, too, Kate. How come you volunteered to take Mike's files if you thought there was something funny about his death?"

"Maybe I like to read," she said.

"Did you?"

"A little."

"Find out anything?"

"Not much."

He shook his head. "I sure hope you're never assigned to interview yourself. You're a tough clam to crack."

"If you want an aria, it'll cost you more than soup and salad," she said as the waiter came prancing over with a tray.

"And you call us mercenary!" he said, watching the plates as they were placed on the table and then digging into his chili with a hungry gusto.

They both concentrated on their food for a minute or two. Then she said, "Look, Radkin, I'm not holding out on you if that's what you think. I knew Mike was really involved in his story, but where it was leading him is something I couldn't say."

He stopped the movement of his spoon long enough to mutter: "I'd find that easier to believe if you were a little piece of fluff . . ."

"What do you mean by that?" she asked, methodically dissecting a roll with her knife.

"Just that you're a journalist, too. I doubt if you and Mike only talked about the weather after you finished having sex."

She opened her eyes very wide and stared at him in amazement. "You certainly don't mince your words, do you,

Radkin? I'd be interested in knowing how many teeth you have left inside your face."

"I say what I mean. Do you?"

"I mean what I say. Who the hell gave you the right to talk to me like that?"

He shrugged and went back to his chili. "Enjoy your soup."

Keeping her eyes fixed on him, she again picked up her knife. For a moment he didn't know whether it was meant for him or the butter. "You're not going to go away, are you?" she said.

"Not for a while."

She buttered her roll and then let out a long, extended sigh, like a steam engine coming to a stop. "All right, I'll be straight with you," she said. "I don't give a shit about that Maybrick woman. As far as I'm concerned, let her rest in peace. But I am interested in Lavinia Chancellor. I think she got a raw deal. She's as guilty of murder as you are of modesty."

"So you were helping Mike with his story, right?"

"Wrong. The way I saw it, he was helping me."

"What's the problem then? Why don't we just bury the hatchet? Maybe we can help each other out."

"The problem, Radkin, is a lack of trust, a lack of communication and a lack of desire."

He lit a cigarette. "That's a lot of lacks."

"There's something else I wouldn't mind lacking," she said, making a face.

He grinned. "So why don't we team up?"

She shook her head. "It wouldn't work."

"Why not?"

"Because we'd probably end up in bed and I don't fancy you."

"Well, we could put a clause in the contract."

"I don't believe in contracts."

"Neither do I."

"Let me have a cigarette," she said, pushing the remnants of her food away and holding out her hand.

He gave her the pack and offered her a light. She inhaled

35

deeply and then looked away, letting the smoke trail out of her mouth. Then she looked back at him and said, "I met her dad the other day . . ."

"Whose dad?"

"Lavinia Chancellor's. His name's Ron. He used to be a cop up in Manchester."

"Used to be? What happened?"

She shrugged. "I just know he retired from the force. I don't like cops, ex or otherwise, but Ron's not a bad bloke."

"What's he feel about his daughter being locked up for twenty years?" asked Joseph.

"That's a pretty dumb question, Radkin," she said. "How the hell would you feel?"

"If I was a cop, I suppose my feelings would be mixed. I guess it depends on whether or not I thought she done it."

"Well he doesn't think she done it."

"Does he have any proof?"

"No proof. Just a lot of unanswered queries. Like why she would have murdered Fry with strychnine and how she got hold of it in the first place."

"How did the prosecution answer that at the trial?"

"Not very well, as far as I can see. They found a chemist who swore she came around to his pharmacy asking for strychnine to kill some rats. When he told her that strychnine was a prohibited poison, she left."

"That's all?"

"That's all they needed, Radkin. They established a motive — Fry was a notorious womanizer and he could be brutal as well. And they established intent — Lavinia didn't hide her feelings about him. The chemist who identified her just tied the circumstantial knot."

"And for that she got twenty years in jail?"

"Twenty years? That's not much. Not too long ago the woman would have hanged! There are plenty around today who wouldn't mind seeing her strung up by a rope."

"You telling me this . . . does it mean you've changed your mind?"

36

She stubbed her cigarette out in her plate. "What it means is that you're on probation for thirty days."

The wind was gusting as they walked back, taking the path along the heath. The leaves were rustling in the night like paper shadows playing timpani in *Fantasia*.

"That's the park that Constable painted, isn't it?" asked Joseph.

"If it is, I don't think he painted it on a night like this," she said.

He tried gazing into the darkness, through the howling woods up into the grassy knolls. "Everybody always says how safe it is here. Nobody talks about muggings like in New York."

"People get mugged here, too," she said, "and murdered and raped. They're just not as loud about it though."

"Statistically, England is still one of the safest places around, I read."

The wind had pushed her hair in front of her face, covering her eyes. She was trying, vainly, to brush it back. "I suppose it depends on what you mean by 'safe'. People here are certainly under control."

He looked over at her. "Do you really think Mike was murdered?" he asked.

"I don't think it was a simple case of hit and run," she replied.

"What made you suspect that maybe he was bumped off?"

"Two things. He'd been making some inquiries into another case . . ."

"What case was that?"

"I don't know. I hadn't seen him for a few days. Then I got a call. He told me he was onto something hot and that he'd see me soon."

"What else?"

"The inquest. There was some evidence that his death might have been from other causes."

"What kind of evidence?"

37

"Things like unexplained markings on his legs and wrists."

"What was the final verdict?"

"Accidental death."

"Which you don't believe."

She glanced at him sideways and he caught a strange look that he hadn't seen in her before.

She quickened her pace and headed for a bench. When she reached it, she sat down. He sat down beside her. She didn't look at him, but stared into the darkness as she said, "There's a funeral service for Mike tomorrow."

"Where?"

"At the cemetery. His mother managed to get him a little plot in Hampstead, in the churchyard at the top of the hill where a lot of the artists are buried."

"Sounds like the perfect place for him to write his play."

She looked at him with her enormous eyes and said, "You don't have much respect for the dead, do you, Radkin?"

"No," he replied. "But I do have some respect for the living."

She reached inside her oversized bag, took out a blue folder and handed it to him.

"What's this?" he asked.

"It's something I found in my desk," she said. "I don't know how it got there."

He glanced at the heading on the folder which read "The Maybrick Case". He looked back at her. "Thanks."

"Tell me something, Radkin," she replied. "Do you think your wife and kids would thank me, too?"

Back at his new-found digs, and through the front door, it suddenly hit him like a ton of quick-drying cement. Some people call it jet lag; others just call it the pits. Whatever, it's that massive discontinuity of time and space that happens when you get someplace too fast. It started by his legs stiffening as he was going up the stairs. To get his feet from one step to another became a test of strength, like climbing to the top of Mont Blanc wearing concrete slippers. He had passed the witching hour. The hands of his internal clock were grinding to a stop.

He had heard the door on the bottom landing squeak open; a sliver of light shone into the hall. As he managed, triumphantly, to move his body onto the next landing, he felt her eyes piercing his back.

He heard her voice without actually seeing her form.

"There's something I left for you by your door, Mr Radkin," she said.

"Can I sleep on it, I hope?"

"It's your colleague's shirt. I found it when I cleaned up. I sewed a button on."

He tried to bring his body up another step. "I'm sure he'd appreciate it . . ."

"There was something in the pocket. I wrapped it up. It's for his poor mother."

"Of course." Somehow he found the strength to lift himself up another step again. "His poor mother . . . I'll see that she gets it, Mrs White."

"That would be very kind, Mr Radkin. It could be something for the dear woman to remember him by," he heard the voice say as the downstairs door squeaked shut.

His room was as cold as an unheated tomb in Siberia, he thought as he let himself in. He headed for the electric fire to turn it on. As he knelt, he felt something in his body crack. "Please God," he muttered to himself, "not my sacroiliac!" And reaching, painfully, to turn on the fire, he suddenly heard another sound, though not from him. This one was a click. And then the lights went out.

Chapter 5

It was late the next morning when he opened his eyes and found himself huddled, stone cold, with the unfunctioning electric heater in his arms. He managed to get up and drop himself onto the couch. He lay there a minute trying to figure out where the hell he was. And as the events of yesterday slowly drifted back into his consciousness, he brought himself up the stairs again to the moment of the click. He blinked his eyes, let out a moan and tried to rub some warmth into his bones. Then he stood up, reached inside the pocket of his slacks, pulled out some coins and went to feed the empty electricity meter.

He was half-way there when he decided that his first stop of the morning should probably be the loo. On the other hand, the sooner he put in the money for electricity, the sooner he could heat the place up. The decision, however, was made for him when the telephone rang. He groaned again, put the change back in his trousers and went to pick up the receiver. It was Kate.

"What's up?" he said, feeling the swell within his bladder becoming more intense.

She sounded almost pleasant. "I forgot to give you the details about the funeral service for Mike," she said.

"I'm not nuts about funerals," he replied while crossing his legs.

"I thought he was your mate."

"He was when he was alive."

"Suit yourself," she said. "I just assumed you might want a chance to meet his mother."

He put his hand down by his crotch and squeezed.

"Radkin?"

"Yeah. What time?"

"It's at five."

"You going too?"

"Yes, but I'll be out most of the day. If you want, I'll meet you at the Everyman Café."

"Where's that?"

"At the top of Hampstead High Street. We passed it yesterday. It's underneath the cinema. Say around half-four."

"Half-four is two where I come from."

He could feel traces of yesterday's hostility as she said, "You're in England now."

"Oh, yeah. I almost forgot."

By the time he hung up the phone he didn't think he could make it to the bathroom one floor below. He tried to consider Mrs White's reaction as he hopped into the kitchen, unzipped his trousers and pissed in the sink. It was one of those things, like masturbating in a confession box while talking to a priest, that gave life its little thrills he felt.

He let the water run a bit before sticking his head under the tap in a futile attempt to clean out his brain. He found a dish- towel and rubbed his hair. Sacrilege always made him hungry. He looked around. There wasn't much for break-fast. Just a kettle with a plug and some "flo-thro" tea-bags marked "PG".

He boiled the water and made some tepid stuff in a silly-looking mug with nineteen yellow bananas painted on. He brought the banana mug back inside the living-room and sat down at his desk. He took a sip, made a face, and thought a bit. Then he went back to the doorway where he had dropped the folder Kate had given him last night on top of Mike's old shirt and the little package Mrs White had made for Mike's mother containing the contents of the pocket. Picking up the stuff, he tossed Mike's shirt into a corner, put the packet into his trousers and took the blue folder over to the desk where he opened it up and began to page through. After a quick inspection, he took a fresh sheet of paper and wrote down what he found:

41

Blue folder. The Maybrick Case: Inventory.

1. Listing from *Reader's Guide 1890–99* on Maybrick case.
2. Listing of books on Maybrick case.
3. Chronology.
4. Notes on Helen Densmore article: "The Maybrick Case."
5. Photostat of cover — penny dreadful entitled: "Guilty or Not Guilty? A Thrilling Romance of Real Life!" In center of page a picture of somber woman in mourning dress with subscript: "Mrs Maybrick as she appeared in court."
6. The beginnings of handwritten manuscript (screenplay?) — *The Trials of Mrs Maybrick* by Michael Rose.
7. Photostats of newspaper articles from *Pall Mall Gazette*, Mar-June, 1889.
8. Notes on readings about Victorian women.
9. A photostat from *Review of Reviews, 1892.* Article entitled: "Ought Mrs Maybrick to be Tortured to Death?"
10. Photostat of article entitled: "The English Dreyfus Case."
11. List of characters, Maybrick story. (3 pages).
12. Photostat of letters to editor concerning Maybrick case. Various newspapers.
13. Photostat of Leading Article from *The Times*, August 8, 1889.
14. Notes on Victorian crime and punishment.
15. Notes on article by Bruno Bettelheim about psychodynamics of prison life.
16. Photostat of page from biography of H. G. Wells with quote underlined: "Nothing changes in England because people who want to alter the order of things change their opinions and attitudes before they change anything else."

After he finished writing the inventory, he went through the papers again and pulled out the *Times* leader, which he then read:

"After a trial lasting seven days, the Liverpool jury have found Mrs Maybrick guilty of the crime of poisoning her husband. We are probably safe in declaring that out of the hundreds of thousands of persons who have followed this case with eager interest and attention, not one in three was prepared for this verdict. The large majority believed that in the presence of so much contradictory evidence the jury would give the prisoner the benefit of the doubt and bring in a verdict as much like the Scottish 'Not Proven' as permitted by our English law. It has not been so. The jury who have seen, it must be remembered, the demeanour of the witness, and have followed the case throughout with patience and anxious attention, have declared that Mrs Maybrick is guilty; and sentence of death has been pronounced upon her. The effect will be to increase the interest which has been felt throughout the country and especially in Lancashire, in the case and the accused . . ."

He put down the photostat for a moment and went to fetch a cigarette. He found a pack in the pocket of his jacket, still strewn on a kitchen chair. On the way back to the living-room he stopped off at the electricity meter and stuck a few coins in. The heater clicked on. He placed it by the desk, lit a smoke, and then continued to read:

"There is always a strange attraction in poisoning cases, different from that which belongs to other investigations of murder. Almost always they imply some drastic treason, for it is only a member of a man's own household, or an intimate friend, that has the opportunities of close intercourse which a case of poisoning commonly implies. Hence the special and tragic interest of such charges. With this come the doubts and conflicts of testimony between experts, the minute scale of the whole thing — for often it is a question of a quarter or a tenth of a grain — so it is not in human nature not to feel a keen and painful curiosity, as the trial proceeds, as to what will be the

43

end. Trials for poisoning are rare, though some doctors say that deaths by poisoning are by no means rare. The poisons that everyone knows about — arsenic, strychnine, and some others — are easy to recognize by their symptoms or their traces so the vulgar murderer is afraid to use them . . ."

He put the paper down again and took a long puff at his cigarette, letting the smoke slowly trail out again and watching it curl upwards toward the ceiling. After a moment or two of blankness, he stood, reached into his trousers and took out the tiny packet Mrs White had made for Mike's mother. He opened it and found a small black diary. He flipped through the pages. It was one of those thick little jobs that gave a page for every day. Mike's scribbles weren't easy to decipher, but it was clear that he had used this book not only as a reminder of his schedule but to keep some cryptic notes. It was a London diary, with some tiny maps in the back and a color-coded plan of the underground which Joseph figured might eventually come in handy. He also decided that Mike had bought it recently since only a few weeks worth of pages had been used.

The early notations seemed fairly insignificant, having to do with bank, digs, West and mother. About a week on there was a reference to BM, Bloomsbury and some sort of reference number — 6495aa56. Then some other things, clearly irrelevant enough to ignore, and then a name, "Beatrice Kendal, solicitor". The next day, an appointment with someone named McIssacs. Underneath was a notation, "2 p.m., Bar Italia". A date had been crossed out and another one inserted which was several days after Mike had died. Then another name, underlined in red, "Dr S.". A few days after that a notation, "East End Books. Whitechapel". And then another name — "Lipski" — also underlined in red. The next day, "Cambridge — R.R.S., Trinity". And, on the bottom, a listing from before — "Dr S." — only this time with an exclamation point.

He turned to the next page. It was the last with any markings and, Joseph realized, was the day of Mike's death. There were three entries: the first was "H.T. — 10 a.m.". After that, in a different colored pen, was written the code from before,

44

followed by a notation, "p101". And underneath, in pencil, was scrawled the last notation, "4th Race — Newmarket. Meet H-g".

He put down the diary and looked up a number in the telephone directory. Then he dialed, hoping she was still there. He was in luck:

"Hi, Kate. It's me, the resident Yank."

"I was just at the door. Is it urgent?"

"No, not really. But since you're on the line, maybe you could tell me who Beatrice Kendal is?".

"She's Lavinia Chancellor's solicitor. A real gem!"

"How about someone called McIssacs?"

"Never heard of him."

"What would BM, Bloomsbury mean followed by a code number."

"Sounds like a book at the British Museum." There was a short silence. Then she said, "This have anything to do with Mike?"

"Maybe."

"You found something in his room?"

"No. Something found me."

"Hope it doesn't bite."

"Can't really bite — ain't got no teeth. See you at two times two plus thirty."

"You are very peculiar, aren't you?"

"Just having some fun."

"Save it for your magazine," she replied.

Beatrice Kendal wasn't in. And according to her chatty secretary, she wasn't going to be.

"It's just one of those days," said the beleaguered voice. "Committee meetings at the Commons, a lecture at two and the Civil Liberties Board convenes at four. I can make an appointment for you next week though . . ."

"Next week the world might end," said Joseph.

"Where did you read that?" groaned the voice. "Never mind. Just don't tell it to Bea. She might start a committee."

"You mentioned a lecture," said Joseph. "Where would that be?"

"'Immigration Rights and Wrongs'? Let's see. I think it's at Bloomsbury House." He could hear the rustling of paper. "Yes, Bloomsbury House."

"Is that near the British Museum?"

"Not far."

"Thanks," he said.

He had just put down the receiver when the telephone rang. He picked it up again.

"Mr Rose?"

"Who's calling?" asked Joseph.

The man said his name. It sounded to Joseph like "Sink". "Is it possible for us to meet today?" he said in an accent that Joseph thought was Indian. The voice sounded urgent.

"I could meet with you," said Joseph, "but . . ."

"You told no one? You did promise, Mr Rose."

"I can vouch for that," said Joseph. "Listen . . ."

"I know you are a busy man, Mr Rose," said the voice, "but something has happened. I must see you at once."

Joseph glanced at his watch. "I'm free this morning. I've got an appointment in Bloomsbury at two."

"There is a little square where Shaftesbury Avenue meets High Holborn Road. I will be there in an hour."

"Wait!" Joseph shouted into the receiver. "Don't hang up!" But it was too late. Whoever it was had already done it.

There was a horrendous buzzing in the hallway that made him wince as he walked down the stairs. It sounded to him as if some madman with a chainsaw had decided, for whatever reason madmen with chainsaws do, to slice the place in half.

On the bottom landing he saw her, kerchief tied around her brittle hair, polka-dotted smock knotted around her waist, an upright vacuum cleaner in her hands, mercilessly sucking up microparticles of dust.

She looked at him — or, rather, his rumpled clothes — as he

tried to squeeze past her in the hall. She turned off the infernal machine to say, "And did you sleep well, Mr Radkin?"

"Very well, Mrs White." He gave her a phony smile.

Her eyes seemed to vacuum him, too, as they ran across his body. "I didn't notice you having any luggage, Mr Radkin . . ."

He pointed to the door. "It's still at the station, Mrs White. I'm collecting it today."

She looked unconvinced as she turned the Hoover back on. "Well, good day to you, then."

"And a very disinfected day to you, too, Mrs White," he said, opening the door and going out.

He took a bus to Piccadilly Circus and then walked up Shaftesbury Avenue to where it met High Holborn.

The square was more like a concrete triangle, he thought — one of those little urban breathing spaces, an island in a sea of cars. There were a few benches, mainly for the neighborhood drunks, and a bank of telephones. Other than that, there wasn't much.

Joseph checked his watch. It had been an hour since the call. He glanced at the people sitting on the benches. A few panhandlers were camping out on one. Another had an elderly gentleman reading *The Times* as its occupant. The third was still vacant.

Walking over to the guy reading the daily, Joseph sat down next to him and said, "Nice day."

The man looked up from his paper and stared Joseph in the mug. "I beg your pardon?" he said.

"Nice day," Joseph repeated. Then, looking up at the sky, he said, "Well, not really. But for here I suppose it is. I mean it's not raining at least. Just a little drizzle but you can't honestly call it rain, can you?"

The man's eyes went back to his paper. "No, I suppose you can't."

"Though it does make things awfully damp," Joseph continued.

"Yes," the man said with some annoyance.

Joseph kept staring at him. "So you didn't phone me, then?"

The man looked up again. "Phone you? Why the devil should I phone you? I don't know you, do I?"

Joseph rubbed his cheek in a pensive gesture and said, "Who knows anybody anymore? I once thought I knew a guy really well. Turns out he got his kicks wearing women's underthings. I found this out one night after he came over the house. When he left, every single pair of Polly's knickers was gone. So did I really know him, I asked myself? Probably not . . ."

The man folded his paper and got up.

"But maybe you know my colleague. His name's Rose. It used to be, anyway. That is to say, he's dead."

The man tucked his paper under his arm and walked away, muttering under his breath, "I do wish they'd finish painting the club . . ."

It was after the elderly gentleman left that Joseph noticed another man, an Indian, thin and, by appearance, rather sensitive, standing by a phone box and glancing nervously about.

Joseph got up from the bench and casually strolled over to where the man was standing.

"Hello," he said.

The man looked at him for a moment, smiled slightly in a manner of someone used to causing no offense, and then began surveying the little square again.

"I'm a colleague of Mike Rose," said Joseph.

The man turned abruptly toward him. He seemed extremely agitated. "But Mr Rose promised that he would say nothing until we agreed the time was right! No one else was to know!"

"Yes, I understand," Joseph began, "but there's a problem . . ."

Suddenly Joseph stopped. He realized the man was no longer listening to him. There was a look of fear in his eyes.

48

Yet he wasn't staring at Joseph, but rather at something beyond.

Turning in the direction the man was looking, Joseph saw a car had stopped by the island in such a way as to block the traffic. It was a fancy jet-black limousine with one-way glass. The cars behind it were blaring their horns, yet the limo stayed there with its engine idling, though no one attempted to get out.

Joseph turned around again to set the guy straight and tell him Rose was dead and that whatever the story was, he could handle it as well. But in that instant the man had left. Joseph spent a few minutes looking for him but the guy had disappeared into the lunch-time crowd. He noticed that the limo, too, had gone.

Going into an empty telephone kiosk, Joseph dialed the operator. He used the credit-card number of *Investigations Magazine* to call West's personal phone. Across the world, it was the middle of the night. He got the answering machine and waited for the beep to make his reply.

"This is Radkin," he said. "There's something fishy here in London town. This morning I got a call from a guy in a lather wanting to speak to Mike. I strung him along, not wanting to scare him off. Couldn't get much from him except that whatever he wanted was urgent. He said his name. Sounded like 'Sink'. He's Indian, I think. Tried to meet him at a rendezvous point, but he pulled a runner. I guess he didn't like my face — or the looks of some fat-ass car. You have any idea what this is about?

"I'm staying at Mike's rooms. The landlady there gave me his diary — so I'm following up some leads. You have my number. It's the same as Mike's. Get back to me when you can . . ."

He hung up the receiver and then pulled Mike's diary out. He flipped through the pages until he found a number. Then he made another call.

"McIssacs here," a voice came through from the other end.

"Hi. This is Joseph Radkin. I'm a friend of Mike's."

"Mike who?"

"Mike Rose. I understand he was to meet you at a place called Bar Italia."

"We did have an appointment. I was wondering what happened to him."

"What happened is he's dead."

"Dead?"

"Yes. That's why he couldn't make it, I guess. I wonder if I could meet you instead?"

"Instead of what?"

"Instead of Mike meeting you. I'm a colleague of his."

"And you're interested in the Maybrick case?"

"Yes. Can we meet sometime today?"

"I suppose . . ."

"You want to try Bar Italia again? By the way — where is it?"

"In Soho. On Frith Street. Near Old Compton Street."

"Noon OK?"

"Let's make it more like three — if you're still alive that is . . ."

Chapter 6

The courtyard entrance of the British Museum on Great Russell Street was filled with the kind of United Nations crowds you see at all international events like circuses and zoos: the same bawling children with chocolate faces and candied hands; the same lost looks; the same dissonant languages searching for an understanding ear; the same schlock of the tired tourist trade. Joseph walked inside and was struck at once by the stale smell of overstuffed museum.

He made his way to the information sign. A young, harried woman looked at him with supersaturated eyes. "The gentleman's toilet is behind you. The café is straight down the hall, left as you came in. The exhibition on Egyptian treasures is shut due to a leak in the roof. Today we close at six."

He stared back at her without responding.

She blinked. "You must want the library then."

He nodded.

"There's a guided tour on the hour. They'll tell you Marx sat in row B, seat number one or row S, seat number ten, depending on who's conducting the tour at the time. But, to be quite honest, they don't know where he sat at all."

"I just want to look at some books," said Joseph.

The woman's expression seemed to slacken into what Joseph saw as sadness, perhaps because her pre-recorded messages were put to waste. She pursed her lips. "I'm afraid it's not so easy then."

"I don't want to borrow them," he assured her.

"Not just anyone can use the museum library, you see."

"No?"

"You need to have a reason."

"Ah," said Joseph. "I do."

51

"Not any reason, mind you. It must be an official reason that can be validated by our staff."

"Just to look at a book?"

The woman raised her eyebrows. "It might be only a book to you, but it's more than that to us. It's part of our national heritage."

"Even if it's a book on twenty ways to milk your cat or using farts in facial creams?"

She stared at him a moment and blinked her eyes again. "I'm speaking of the totality; the fact that every British book ever published is stored in our repository."

"What if I promise to keep my shoes on and wash my hands three times?"

There was that stoic quality about her which clearly said she had been here long enough to have seen almost every type. Even so, she sighed as she pointed to an entrance just several feet away: "Through the swinging doors. First office on your left."

As he went he heard her voice intoning to the next one in the line: "The gentleman's toilet is behind you . . ."

They had been quite pleasant at the admissions office. Of course, as an American journalist working on a story they would be pleased to give him entry. But could he just provide them with a letter corroborating that?

Half the skill of being a decent journalist is knowing how to short-circuit bureaucracy, Joseph never tired of telling his wife. (Polly's reply had always been the same: "Then maybe you can do something about your 350 dollars' worth of accumulated parking fines.") So, once outside again, in the fresher air — if soot and leaded fumes can be called "fresh" — he reached inside his pocket and extracted a folded letter from West he had received the day before he left for England, telling him that even though he would have loved to have paid him in advance for the flight, bookkeeping problems prevented it. Then, ripping off the letterhead which contained the bold logo of *Investigations Magazine*, he brought it to a nearby copy shop and had them run off several pieces of blank stationery. This he took with him to a small café on Museum Street where he scribbled a letter of confirmation to the British Library, Admissions, signing West's name on the bottom.

Reading it over a cup of bitter coffee, he realized this was the first serious piece of writing he had done since he arrived. He folded it neatly and placed it in his notebook, which, in turn, went inside the pocket of his jacket. Then he glanced at his watch. It was well past two. Borrowing a phone directory from the woman behind the counter, he looked up the address of Bloomsbury House. He copied it down and then showed it to her. She said it wasn't far.

Bloomsbury House, in fact, was only a few minutes away. It was one of those great Georgian-type buildings which let in the light the Victorians so detested. He walked up the stairs and opened the door and then went straight over to a table marked "Reception". No one was seated there. But a few feet away, a man in a fraying uniform was mopping the floor.

"I'm looking for Beatrice Kendal," he said, turning to the elderly man who looked back at him blankly. "She's giving a talk."

"There's no lectures today, squire," he said. "Unless you mean the symposium."

"What's it on?" he asked.

"Something to do with wogs, I suspect. It usually is."

He directed Joseph to a room on the second floor. The doors were open, the seats were half filled with well-dressed people, all somewhere in their middle years. Behind a row of tables, looking out at the audience, several tired people sat. He had seen their type before, usually at academic events where the same thing was said over and over again in slightly different ways by slightly different speakers. The lady at the podium was an elderly woman with short springy curls of snow-white hair atop a lovely round face. Her lively, energetic eyes, magnified behind her specs, were in stark contrast to the others seated at the speaker's table, gazing out at the audience, which gazed back, in a curious kind of staring match. She was speaking as Joseph came in the door:

". . . one sometimes forgets that Britain's policy toward immigration was more advanced in the nineteenth century than it is today. From 1823 to 1901 not a single refugee was expelled nor a single one prevented from coming in. And this freedom of entry applied to all foreigners, whether refugees or not: deposed kings and royalists, remnants of revolutionary armies, escapies from prisons, Jews and Huguenots — all gained entry equally, without question. Indeed, it was a source of national pride."

There was a pause as she sized up the effect of her words on her audience. Then she continued in a more impassioned tone, "I ask you to think on this when you consider the plight of those poor, homeless people, uprooted from their native lands, who traveled so many thousands of miles to reach this place of cherished dreams only to be imprisoned by the Home Office on a ship anchored precariously off Harwich. My friends, what terrible cynicism it takes to speak of these people as simply 'economic refugees'. For were we not all children of economic refugees somewhere down the line? Please do consider this. Think of us now and think of us then. And ask yourself: 'How far have we really come?'"

There was a polite scattering of applause as people stood up, grabbed their wraps and prepared to go. Only a few stragglers remained by the time Joseph walked up to the front. He could hear one of the men at the speaker's table saying, "My dear Bea! You were wonderful as always! But the problem is, you see, if you let one in you have to let them all. And where does it end? Half of Asia is already knocking at our door. Heaven knows what will happen when Hong Kong finally goes red. It might be just the start of a torrential flood."

Beatrice Kendal was gathering her papers. She didn't look up as she spoke. "Movement of peoples, my dear Farquhar, has been going on since time began. Believe it or not, they don't all want to spend the rest of their lives in this cold, pneumatic drizzle."

"Ah, but there's the rub, you see. We're a small country, with rather special conditions. You can't take a chap from India who's gone around half naked all his life, eating nothing but rice and ginger, and make an Englishman out of him. Those chaps have a strange enough idea of what they're going to find here. And when they are allowed to stay, they only end up wanting to go home."

She stopped shuffling her papers, pulled her glasses down her nose and looked up at him over the top of the frames. "Farquhar, when your ancestors were living in caves, India was the most civilized nation in the world. The Asian presence in England has been a fact ever since the days when we destroyed their indigenous economies. In lieu of the several trillion pounds in restitution we should have paid them, at least we can welcome those who do us the honor of wanting to come. If your desire is turning the clock back to your lovely colonial romps, please do it in the privacy of your own home."

Farquhar turned and went off with one of the other gentlemen who had been seated at the table. As he left, Joseph heard him say, "She's really quite a delightful old girl when it's not her time of the month, you know . . ."

Joseph saw her struggling with her coat and took the opportunity to come over to her side. "Let me give you a hand," he said, raising the sleeve high enough for her to insert her arm.

"The real problem with old age," she said, twisting her torso in order that the coat could fall in place, "is stiffness of the bone. Your mind is mobile; your body less so."

"You seem to get around OK," said Joseph. "Your secretary gave me a list of twenty places where you'd be — all within a quarter of an hour."

"Dorothy can be a bit of a chatterbox. But she's absolutely indispensable. I don't know what I'd do without her," she said, placing her papers in a scruffy briefcase and closing it up. She gave Joseph a look. "You wanted to see me?"

"I'm a journalist," he said, "a colleague of Mike Rose. I believe he talked with you about the Lavinia Chancellor case. You're her solicitor, I understand."

"You understand correctly, young man. The poor girl was unfortunately stuck with me." She looked down at her watch. "Whatever you have to say, you'd better make it brief. I'm due at the Commons in twenty minutes from now."

"What did Mike want to know?"

"He wanted to know if Lavinia Chancellor had a fair trial."

"Did she?"

"In the sense that our system of justice is a contest between two opposing sides played according to a certain set of rules, I suppose you could call it fair. But if you're asking me whether the trial fairly ascertained the truth, my answer would be no."

Joseph scratched the back of his head — a habit he picked up in his years of interviews when faced with an obfuscated reply that nevertheless seemed to make sense. "How so?" he said.

She looked down at her watch again. "Do you mind if we walk? I really can't be late."

"Sure," he said, following her out the door. "I usually talk when I walk anyway. Most of the time, though, it's to myself."

She gave him a curious look. "What do you know about the case, young man?"

"Not much," he replied, as they went down the stairs. "I know she was convicted of poisoning her lover with cocaine cut with strychnine, some of which was found around the house. And I know there was an eyewitness — a pharmacist who claims she tried to buy the stuff to kill some rats."

"In English law, in order to convict someone of a crime such as murder, one needs to provide a body, a motive, a means of execution and the ability to commit the act. In Lavinia Chancellor's case all this was proven to the satisfaction of the judge . . ." They had reached the pavement. She stopped to wave down a taxi.

"How about the jury?"

"Juries usually take their cues from the highest authority, I've found. In a court of law often the questions which might provide a logical path to the truth are not allowed to be asked — or answered. Truth, you see, isn't always one thing. There's a legal truth, a literal truth, and the truth of life. Often they don't coincide."

"Yes, but this was a simple case of poisoning. Surely the object is to find out if she did it."

"No case is simple, young man. Especially one that involves poisoning." A taxi pulled over to the curb. Bea opened the passenger door and got in. Looking back, she caught his eye. "Ride with me to Parliament, if you like."

"Thanks," he said, sliding in alongside her. He closed the door behind him and the taxi drove off.

"In our system of justice, appearance often means much more than reality. In the Lavinia Chancellor case, for example, what we had was a woman who could have killed her lover. She had the opportunity to kill her lover and she had the means. That much is certain. What was never proven to my satisfaction is whether she actually did kill her Mr Stephen Fry."

"What was the motive if she did?"

"We all have a motive for killing one another, Mr . . ." Suddenly she stopped. "I'm afraid you have the advantage of me . . ."

"I'm sorry," he said, with a smile, "the name's Radkin. Joseph Radkin. I'm from the States."

"The fact that you're American would never have been doubted, even in a court of law, Mr Radkin . . ."

"Joseph, please."

". . . based on your elongation of certain vowels, your awkward grin, your insistence on a trying informality . . ."

"Yes, but back to motives . . ."

". . . and a rather abrupt and dogged nature. But, as you

57

insist, back to motives: Lavinia Chancellor was one of those sad little creatures — all too common in this country — who end up in love with a gentleman sadist. Of course she had a motive, as anyone with broken ribs as well as a broken heart could attest!"

"So Stephen Fry beat her? It's not murder, then, it's self-defence!"

"The rules state that one isn't allowed to defend oneself with strychnine, Mr Radkin."

"But twenty years in jail . . ."

She cut him short. "Power relationships are nearly always punctuated by violence or by threats. Women, supposedly being the weaker sex, have traditionally been one step above children and one below dogs in the beating chain. The idea, be it fact or myth, that poisoning has historically been used as women's court of last resort frightens the willies off the male judiciary. In brief, Mr Radkin, they wouldn't like to be seen encouraging it."

"No. I suppose not. Assuming that she did it, of course. But as far as I can figure out there was only one damning testimony — that of the pharmacist. It was all so circumstantial!"

"Murder usually is. But how does one ascertain the truth, Mr Radkin? Appearances are so often deceiving. Today there are six men and women who have been languishing in prison for years having been convicted of dynamiting a pub and killing many innocent people. The key to their conviction was a test which purported to prove that they had been handling explosives. The fact that this test is disputed by experts who say that a positive result might as easily have been achieved by fingering ordinary playing-cards was dismissed as irrelevant. One authority says yes, another says no. The judge and jury choose which one they wish to believe. But were they responsible for the crime?" She shrugged.

"Surely something like that would be appealed, though."

"Appeal is a long and arduous process which demands

much patience and fortitude during which time one is likely to continue rotting in jail. Even so, there is an extreme reluctance in this country to interfere with a case which seems to have been fairly tried without new and compelling evidence coming to light."

Joseph thought a moment. Then he asked, "How well do you know Lavinia's father?"

"How well would you know anyone who phones you night and day? The answer, I suppose, is quite well and not at all. But he's a rather fascinating and tragic figure, Mr Radkin . . ."

"Tragic? How so?"

"He was a policeman, you understand. It's difficult after all those years to see life from the other side."

"But he believes in his daughter's innocence?"

The taxi had pulled over to the side of the road. She opened up her purse and withdrew a bank-note. "Oh, yes, Mr Radkin, he certainly does."

"You think he's onto anything new that wasn't brought up at the trial?" asked Joseph, with the eagerness of a bloodhound picking up a scent — though in his case it may have been a poodle.

She paid the driver and then turned back to Joseph. "Better than that, Mr Radkin; he has the knowledge that comes from an abiding faith."

Joseph shook his head. "They have a saying where I come from: two bits and faith won't get you in the door if the asking price is four."

"I beg to differ. If you're going to devote your life to a cause, faith is something you can't do without."

"Maybe you're right," said Joseph, "but it would be nice if there was something a little more tangible to go along with it. I'm the kind of guy who likes a little bread with my butter."

"Lavinia's father is a complicated individual," she replied as she made ready to go. "He's a man full of surprises. I have no doubt that in time he'll provide us with 'something a little more'. I only hope that 'something' will be enough to get his daughter through your proverbial door."

She was out of the cab when he rolled down the window. "One other thing. Did you know Mike Rose is dead?"

She turned around. "It happens to the best of us," she said.

Chapter 7

The taxi took him back to the West End. He got out at the corner of Old Compton and Frith Streets.

At first glance Bar Italia was little more than a hole in the wall. Inside, however, the space was doubled by a huge mirror which ran down its length. It was a cheap trick, but it worked. The row of bar stools which were bolted to the floor faced the mirror and a narrow ledge — about the width of a cappuccino cup. When you sat down, you were forced to look yourself in the kisser. If you didn't shave that day or had a bad night, it was better to drink whatever you ordered with your eyes shut.

McIssacs was easy to find. He was the only one who looked like he didn't have a wife and three children waiting for him someplace in Sicily. He was seated midway down the aisle and was wearing a wrinkled corduroy suit, a paisley shirt with a buttoned-down collar and a black fedora pushed back on his head, exposing a forelock of hair that fell over a pair of lively eyes. Joseph figured it had to be him because nobody else but a down-at-the-mouth academic would wear an outfit like that.

Ordering a coffee, Joseph walked over and squeezed himself onto the stool to McIssacs' left and looked at his reflection in the glass.

"Hi," he said with a cheery grin. "You must be McIssacs."

The image in the mirror looked slightly put out. "Must I? How unfortunate. I thought perhaps I could have been someone else."

"Like who, for instance?"

"How about Giancarlo Giannini?"

"Not a chance," Joseph replied.

McIssacs studied his image in the mirror for a moment and then fingered the fedora. "Not even with the hat?"

Joseph shook his head. "They don't wear 'em anymore. Where'd you get it anyway? Salvation Army?"

"Oxfam, actually."

"I figured that. You get the shirt there too?"

McIssacs glanced at his own reflection in the mirror again. "Not the shirt. I got it new in '63."

"I bet," said Joseph.

"Can't afford to throw anything away on my salary."

Joseph took a sip of coffee. "Doesn't bother me. In fact it'll probably be worth a fortune in another couple years." Looking at his cup appreciatively, he said, "Thanks for bringing me here, though. Best cup of java I've tasted since I came to Chill-Ville."

"Glad you approve," said McIssacs. He lifted his glass containing a liquid which looked a little like hair-oil. "I come here for the grappa, myself." He took a sniff of his drink. "I don't really like it. Actually, I don't suppose anyone does. It's just that I'm trying to teach myself Italian."

"It's all right," said Joseph. "You don't have to explain it to me."

McIssacs nodded and looked into the mirror again. "So Rose is dead?"

"Yeah. Any idea what happened to him?"

"No more than you, probably. He came to see me about the Maybrick case."

"Why you?"

"I wrote a book — *The Poisoned Chalice*. You haven't read it, I suppose?"

Joseph shook his head. "So what did you tell him?"

"Nothing that would get him bumped off, if that's what you mean."

"You never know what effect your words might have on someone," said Joseph, taking out a cigarette and lighting up. "I knew a guy once who said 'hello' to someone he met on the street. The other guy looked up to reply and fell through an open manhole."

"I hope that's not the way Rose met his end," said McIssacs, making a sour face.

"No. He got run over by a truck. At least that's what some people say. So what's it about? Your book, that is."

"Victorian poisonings. It was all the rage, you know. Not my book, unfortunately. Poisoning. The fear of it, anyway."

"What do you mean?" asked Joseph.

McIssacs pondered his glass of hair-oil and then pushed it aside. "Some people claim that it was the Victorian alternative to divorce. But, actually, when you count them up, there weren't all that many. Reality, you know, never matches expectations. But the idea certainly was popular."

"The idea?"

"Well, think of it this way — the angel in the house was in charge of the kitchen. And if she got fed up with being angelic, there was nothing stopping her from putting something more than pepper in the soup — except perhaps the image of a few Maybricks being roasted at the cooker."

"But poisonings did happen," said Joseph.

"Yes, but it's a rather curious notion. Maybe you heard the saying: 'One man's meat . . .'"

"Yeah," said Joseph. "But what's the point?"

"Just that whether a substance is poison or not is in the eye of the beholder."

"Or the stomach of the taster," Joseph put in.

"Well, consider homeopathy. They look at poisons in an entirely different way. Anything is toxic once it reaches a certain threshold in one's system. What we commonly consider to be poisons are substances that have a low threshold. But it's all a question of degree."

"Right," said Joseph. "But maybe you could tell me what you're getting at."

"The Maybrick case. Arsenic. What is it? A metallic element. Atomic number thirty-three, to be precise. In the form of arsenic trioxide, or white arsenic, it's been used for centuries as a tonic to increase resistance to fatigue. As far back as Cleopatra's day, women have been rubbing it on their faces to beautify their skin. There's even a famous spa where arsenic is an active ingredient in the waters. And Maybrick, the husband, used it to get high."

"I've been puzzled about that," said Joseph, rubbing the stubble on his chin. "Why arsenic? There must have been safer stimulants around."

"It was the drug of choice among a certain group in those days. Something like cocaine is now amongst your journalist chums," McIssacs said with a wink.

"But why, for Christ's sake? The threshold between drug and poison there is pretty small."

"Not really," said McIssacs. "In fact the threshold gets higher the more you take. Most arsenic-users can eat spoonfuls of the stuff — and the more you eat, the more you crave."

"It still doesn't explain why they chose arsenic." Joseph stubbed his cigarette out and lit another.

"I've got a theory about that. You know how people nowadays are terrified of AIDS? Well, in Maybrick's day the terror that stalked the streets alongside Jack the Ripper was syphilis. It was a plague of devastating proportions. And, of course, those were the days before antibiotics . . ."

"So what's the point?" asked Joseph, impatiently.

"The point is a certain substance in those days was thought to be a preventative against syphilis."

Joseph's nose twitched the way it always did when he felt himself picking up a scent. "Arsenic?"

"The very one."

"So let me get this straight — you're saying that arsenic trioxide wasn't only a powerful stimulant that kept Victorian business going during the day, it was also a sort of male prophylactic that protected the horny little bastards from coming down with the Big 'S' at night. Have I got you right, McIssacs?"

"Well, I might not have put it quite that way, Radkin. But I think you've got the essence."

64

"Jesus!" Joseph exclaimed, his eyes as big as chewy peppermint drops. "Just think what the drug industry could do with that!"

McIssacs looked him straight in the face. "I wouldn't be terribly surprised if they had."

He liked McIssacs. And he would have stayed to talk if he hadn't a funeral to attend.

"Not your own, I trust," McIssacs had said.

"I'll give you a ring," Joseph had replied, getting up to go. "Maybe there's a few things you can help me iron out."

McIssacs had pushed back his errant hair and grinned. "Why not?"

Leaving Bar Italia, Joseph walked down to Leicester Square where he caught a train on the Northern Line. It was a depressing ride. It was even more depressing when he got off.

The bowels of Hampstead tube station had none of the trendy chicness from up above — unless sewers were in this year, and you could never be sure they weren't, he thought; not in times like these when "style" was a buzzword that gave value to things you would otherwise throw away. He followed the signs that led through the tunnels of this dreary underworld till he came to the lift.

Emerging into the Victorian chill of the station, he stopped for a moment to scribble in his notebook: "The sole democratizing force in London, as far as I can tell, is the transportation system. The people in that black hole might not speak to one another but, whether rich or poor, they can all get ill on the same pneumonic plague that snuffed their ancestors over a hundred years before."

The Everyman Cinema was just across the street. It had a simple marquee without razmataz and plain, cheaply printed posters advertising some esoteric film that movie buffs collect like stamps. On the side was a small courtyard with a hand-painted sign suspended from an archway, directing him down a flight of stairs. Again he began his descent; this time, however, it was only one floor below the surface of the earth's crust and, compared to the subway, not bad at all.

He recognized the syncopated rhythms of the Dave Brubeck Quartet as he pushed open the smoky glass doors and walked into the room. It could have been Chicago — maybe 1965. He looked over at the bar. She was sitting there on a stool, her legs crossed to the side, a bottle of Beck's in her hand and a cigarette in her mouth. She didn't look too happy; but he would have been the first to admit that happiness wasn't everything. There was a sweet sense of blues about her, like Juliette Greco in her better days, He went over and sat down.

"Hi. I didn't expect to find you in a place like this."

She looked at him. He could tell she'd had maybe one or two before he came. "Is that a variation on 'What's a nice girl like you . . . et cetera?'"

He lit a cigarette. "Nice girls don't exist; they're just a figment created by the church as a form of psychological birth control."

"It's just like a man to use the words 'nice', 'girl' and 'church' in the same sentence and somehow make it sound nasty."

"Well, at least we're making progress," he said, signaling the bartender to bring another beer. "I've gone from being the generic Yank to the generic man."

She took a swig of her Beck's and followed it with a tobacco chaser. "Put a lid on it, Radkin. I've had a hard day."

He scratched his head. It was itching him like crazy these days. He considered the idea that maybe he had lice. What would Mrs White think, he wondered, if she found out he was infesting her sheets. "I thought we got past all this yesterday, Kate."

"Yesterday was the day before I had a run-in with my editor," she said.

"I can relate to that." He lifted the beer that the bartender brought him and took a thirsty drink. Then, using the back of his hand to wipe his mouth, he said, "What's it about?"

66

"My article — women in prison. The little toad says it's got too much periphery and not enough center, whatever that means."

He took another drink. "Not enough meat?"

"Too much meat; not enough bone." She looked him in the eye. "Do you know that prison staff in this country have to sign the Official Secrets Act?"

"Yeah, well I'm not surprised. Prisons are places we're supposed to know nothing about because if we knew what went on inside we'd probably tear 'em all down and then where would they be?"

"When Holloway Prison was built in 1852 it had a sign above the gate that said: 'May God Preserve the City of London and Make This Place a Terror to Evil-Doers.' As far as I can tell, things haven't changed a bit since then."

"Holloway — that's where Lavinia Chancellor is locked up, right?"

"Yeah, it's the women's prison. If you're convicted you're either sent there or to Styal. But a good number of women kept there haven't even gone to trial. Most of them are on remand. There's a wing known as C–1, it's the psychiatric unit where women are sent for observation. I went there the other day on a press tour set up by the Howard League for Penal Reform. The first thing you hear when you come near the wing is a low, moaning sound — something like a dirge. As you get closer, the moans become wails. Finally, when you're inside, the wails become pitiful screams. The feeling of misery that permeates the place couldn't have been worse in a nineteenth-century asylum. The day before, I heard that a woman had slashed her wrists. She'd barricaded herself in her cell, wrenched the basin from the wall and had smashed it against the floor until she had enough of a jagged edge to mutilate herself. You could still see traces of blood on the floor."

Joseph made a face of disgust. "You mean they couldn't even be bothered to do a proper job of mopping up?"

"Things like that aren't unusual," she went on. "They

happen all the time. In men's prisons the tension builds up and they start to kill each other. The women direct their violence against themselves. In either case, there just aren't enough staff to run the place; most of the warders are kept busy taking remand prisoners back and forth to the Old Bailey."

"So how the hell do they keep any order at all?"

"Simple." She looked at him hard, took a final swig of beer and said, "Drug the hell out of them!"

The drizzle had started again by the time they left. The cemetery wasn't far; a few yards down the hill and then a dog-leg to the right.

"You ever have a chance to interview Lavinia Chancellor?" he asked her as they strolled.

The mist had settled on her hair like tiny droplets of dew; her hands were deep inside the pockets of her mackintosh. She looked cold and waif-like as she said, "I haven't been able to arrange it yet. You can't just walk in there, you know . . ."

In the near distance he could see the church, shrouded in white as if specially for the occasion. To the right, the iron fence of the graveyard came into view. It was almost pleasant, he thought: so quiet and serene. He could understand how a mother wouldn't mind burying her son up there — if she could afford it.

As they walked inside the leafy entrance he noticed the gravestones. "There are some important names chiseled into these hunks of rock," he said with a note of surprise.

"I know," said Kate. "Artists, writers, statesmen . . . Mike probably feels like he made it at last."

He looked toward the far side of the cemetery where a small group of people were standing behind a mound of freshly dug dirt. "How the hell did she do it?" he asked. "There must be a waiting list at least a hundred years long."

"I'll tell you how — she paid someone to give up their space, that's how! If you have money, you can do anything! Most people just get thrown in a ditch!"

Joseph shrugged. "I don't really care what they do to me," he said, "as long as they don't grind me up and sell me in a fast-food café."

She looked at him. "A man of great ambition."

"My ambition is not to die at all."

"Yeah, I'm sure that's what most Americans would say. Well, good luck."

He let out a chuckle and watched his breath vaporize in the air. Through the haze he saw a man nod his head in their direction. He was standing off to the side a yard or two away from the rest of the assembly, holding the tiny hand of a young girl.

"Who's that guy over there?" asked Joseph.

"That's Ron Chancellor. The kid is Lavinia's little girl."

"I thought as much," said Joseph. "He looks like a cop."

"The woman to the left of the vicar is Mike's mum."

"The one dressed in black, wearing a veil? A blind man could have spotted her. She reeks of diamonds and French perfume — even from over here." He looked at Kate. "You recognize anyone else?"

She shook her head. "No."

They waited at a respectful distance as the vicar finished his ashes-to-ashes, dust-to-dust routine. Then as the condolence line began to form up, they made their way over to the grave.

"I think I'll have a chat with Ron," she said, moving off to the side.

"Catch up with you later," Joseph called back. "I just want to say a few words to Mike's mom."

He got into place at the end of the condolence line and, as it slowly moved forward, he searched through his pocket for a card. The only thing handy was a dry-cleaning tag that he couldn't find when he had gone to pick up his only suit a day before his flight departed. He scribbled his name and phone number on the back and put the pen away just in time to meet the lady with the black moustache.

"My deepest sympathies," he said, standing somewhat awkwardly and unsure of whether to take her hand.

"Thank you."

"He was my friend."

She looked at him through her veil, curled slightly above her lip. He could hardly make out her face. "I don't think I know you. Do I?" she said.

"No. That is, I don't think you do. I worked with your son on *Investigations Magazine*. You see . . . um . . . I'm taking his place."

"Oh."

"Not his place, exactly. I could never do that." He laughed nervously. "Mike was too — how shall I put it? — unique."

"Yes . . ."

"You know what I mean?"

"Quite . . ."

"Of course you do. After all, you're his mom . . . or were . . ."

"Was there something you wanted to say, Mr . . ." She lifted up her veil. She had magnificent eyes, he thought.

"Radkin. Joseph."

"Mr Radkin Joseph."

"No . . . that is . . . my name. It's Joseph Radkin. Not Radkin Joseph." He handed her the card. "Here."

She looked at the crumpled paper in her hands and tried to make sense of it. "This seems to be a slip from a dry-cleaning shop."

He gave her a silly grin and made a motion with his hand. "On the other side . . ."

She turned the slip over. "Oh, I see."

"My phone number. In case you want to talk . . ."

"About what?"

"About Mike. About his life. About his death."

"My son was run over, Mr Radkin," she said. Her voice had suddenly gained a more aristocratic ring. "He was hit by a truck. His life was crushed out of him before anyone had a chance to recognize who he really was."

"Most people die before they're truly recognized,

70

Mrs Hughes," he said. "But I can assure you, he did make his mark on the world."

The harshness melted as tears came to her eyes. "He had so much to give. Now they've taken him away."

"Who took him away?" asked Joseph.

She shook her head and wiped the tears from her eyes.

"Virginia?" It was a deep male voice with enough authority to make them both turn in its direction. The speaker was a middle-aged man in a cashmere coat who could have stepped out of a single-malt whisky ad. He had a no-nonsense look in his eyes. "Could we go now?"

Her face, which had become somewhat flustered, suddenly took on a mannered expression again. "Yes. Of course, Cecil," she said. And, without turning back to Joseph, she and the cashmere coat quickly walked away.

It was at that moment he heard another voice, more familiar now. "Radkin, there's someone I'd like you to meet."

Joseph turned and saw Kate. The tough-looking man was walking up behind her, granddaughter in tow.

"Mr Chancellor, I presume," Joseph said in a Holmsean voice.

"Let's get out of here," the tough man said. "I need a drink."

As they walked from the cemetery, Joseph noticed a black limo with mirrored glass, parked by the gate, start up and drive away.

Chapter 8

They were sitting in the garden of a pub adjacent to the heath. Chancellor was on his second pint of beer. His granddaughter was sucking cola from a straw. Joseph was nursing a whisky splashed on ice. Kate had gone home to pick up her son.

Chancellor put down his glass and looked across the table at Joseph. He narrowed his eyes. "I don't like reporters," he said.

"I'm sure you have your reasons," Joseph replied.

The ex-cop looked at the little girl who had been watching them intently ever since they had sat down. He pointed toward a children's play area and said, "Jemima, do you see the slide and swings?"

She continued to stare at him with her huge dark eyes.

"Wouldn't you like to play over there?"

She shook her head.

"You can watch us from there just as well."

She stared at him a moment more and then slid down from her chair and walked slowly over to a swing where she sat motionlessly and fixed them in her gaze once again.

Chancellor took another drink. "As long as she sees me, she's OK."

"You're looking after her yourself?" asked Joseph.

"She's in a home," Chancellor replied. "I take her out occasionally."

"What about your wife?"

"She'll have been dead ten years, tomorrow."

His eyes, Joseph thought, were like stone. "You're from Manchester?" he asked.

"Yeah."

"That's not far from Liverpool . . ."

"About thirty miles. Liverpool's the port. Used to be a great city . . . once upon a time."

Joseph rubbed the side of his face. "Are you familiar with the Maybrick case?"

He took out a pouch of tobacco and some papers and began to roll his own. "I don't like the idea, Radkin . . ."

"What idea?"

"Mixing the two together."

"Why not?"

He put the paper cylinder to his lips and licked the edge. "It muddies the waters."

"It can also create a climate of sympathy and pressure for an appeal."

He lit up and then reached into his jacket pocket and pulled out some folded clippings. "I carry these around with me," he said, handing them over to Joseph. "When I get tired, I give them a read. It's like taking a bath in filth. It pumps up my adrenalin again."

Joseph glanced through the articles. They were mainly from the tabloids, all with bold, sensational headlines and all with the same voluptuous picture worked in.

"This your daughter?" asked Joseph.

"You know where they got that picture?" he said. "When she was at university, she was in a play. She was supposed to be a lusty barmaid . . ." He reached into his pocket again and took out a glossy photo. "Lavinia could never really get into the part — she kept trying to play it like a French courtesan." His eyes narrowed again as he handed the photo to Joseph. The picture was of a dolled-up Lavinia standing between two young men on the stage of a theatre set. "It's from a publicity release. They just took a pair of scissors and cut her out so she'd look like a whore."

Joseph shoved the articles back across the table. "But these are just scandal sheets!"

"Ten or fifteen million readers, if you add up the combined circulation," he said, folding the clippings neatly and putting them back in his pocket. He left the photo on the table.

"How about the serious press?"

Chancellor leaned slightly forward. Joseph could see little beads of sweat forming on his brow. "Listen, Radkin," he said, "I used to be a policeman. I know how it's done. You can put anybody's life underneath a microscope and find some lice — and I mean anyone!"

He automatically felt the itch on his head. To sublimate the desire to scratch it, he took out a cigarette from his pack and lit up. "I'm not that kind of journalist."

"Maybe not. Anyway, your friend Rose was better than most, I'll say that for him."

"You talked with him much?"

"We had our understanding."

"Meaning?"

"He gave a few things to me, I gave a few things to him."

"Like what?"

His face was like steel. Poker would have been his game, Joseph thought.

"Bits and pieces."

"Tell me about Stephen Fry."

There was a little vein in Chancellor's temple that began to throb at the mention of the name. "What do you want to know?"

Joseph shrugged. "How did they meet? What was he like?"

"They met at university." He pointed to the publicity shot. "That's him standing to Lavinia's right."

Joseph picked up the photo again and inspected it. The young Fry was slim, pimply and dirty blond. He had a ridiculous expression on his face. It was the other young man in the picture who seemed more in control. He had that certain look of public-school arrogance which guaranteed several unpaid tailor bills and someone's cheap abortion by the age of twenty-one.

"Who's the toff?" asked Joseph, pointing to the bigger man in the photo.

"That's Reginald Palmerston before he wore his trousers

long. You'd know him if you read the Tory press. He's being touted for a major cabinet post one of these days."

"What does he do otherwise?"

"Sons of High Court judges don't need to do much in this country, Radkin, except wait for a solid constituency to open up."

"So Fry and Palmerston were buddies back then, huh?"

"Fry was of a different class. But he hung around Palmerston's set — at least for a while."

"What was Fry's profession after he left school?"

Chancellor let out a short, ironic laugh. "Philanderer."

"You need a college degree for that?"

"Fry didn't get a degree — unless they give one in fornication."

Joseph looked over at the raven-haired, dark-eyed child seated on the swing. "Was Fry the father?" He made a small gesture toward her.

He nodded. "That was the claim. But I don't see anything of him in her."

"Neither do I," said Joseph, glancing at the exotic-looking young woman in the photo again. He looked back at the cop. "They lived in Chelsea. That's a pretty rich part of town."

"A little too rich for my tastes . . ."

"Some of her friends testified that Fry made her life so miserable that it's little wonder she killed him. How come she didn't just walk out?"

"You tell me," he said, with a trace of anger in his voice. Regaining his calm, he added, "She did. Several times. She always went back though."

"Why?"

"Not through any encouragement of mine."

"Money?"

"I told her I'd give her money if she needed it. Besides, Fry was always broke."

"Love?"

"Maybe a kind of love . . ." There was a peculiar look in his eyes. "The kind that's just the other side of hate."

Joseph stared at him, this lean, tough man, this former cop, and wondered why he sympathized. His voice was softer. "How do you know she didn't do it?"

He looked over at the little girl. "Because she told me so. That's why."

"Is that enough?"

"For me it is."

"Not for the courts, though." Joseph said.

Chancellor stubbed out his smoke in the ashtray. Then he looked back at Joseph. "How well did you know your friend?"

"Mike? Not very well."

"Kate says you're staying in his place."

"That's right."

He stared at him more intently. "Find anything there?"

"Not much. Did Kate tell you about the stuff that was stolen from her house?"

He nodded.

"You think it could have been the police?"

"Could have been. But it's not their style. If they wanted it, all they had to do was ask."

"Who then?"

"I'll see what I can find out." He got up from his chair and, as he did, Jemima jumped down from the swing and ran over to his side. "I'll give you my number," he said, tearing out a page from a small diary he carried in his vest.

"You're living in London now?" asked Joseph putting the slip inside his wallet.

"We've got a room on Burghley Road — in Tufnell Park."

"That's around where Holloway Prison is located, isn't it?"

Chancellor reached down and took the little girl's hand. "It's not too far away from there."

He caught the underground and picked up his stuff at Victoria Station. The return trip took him over an hour. He felt exhausted as he dragged his luggage up the stairs. At the second landing he could hear his telephone start to ring. He dropped the scruffy valise, reinforced with rope, on the landing and ran up the last flight of stairs. He was huffing and puffing as he picked up the receiver and shouted down the line: "Hello!"

"Hi!" He recognized the cheery voice at once. "How's it goin', pal!"

"Fine, if you don't mind being bathed in gloom. What's the weather like back there, West?"

"Sunny and warm. It's a mint-julep sort of day, I'd say."

Joseph groaned.

"You don't like foggy London town?"

"The fog wouldn't be so bad; it's the chill in your bone that gets me."

"Try wearing long undies — that's what the natives do, I understand."

"Thanks for the advice."

"So you suspect Mike wasn't hit by a truck . . ."

"Oh, I can vouch for that, all right. I was just at his funeral. The question, I gather, is whether it was the truck that killed him or if he was already dead."

"You got anything hard?"

"Nope. You know his files were stolen, though . . ."

"By whom?"

"Wish I knew."

"If he was set up, I want to know about it, Radkin."

"Did Rose say anything about that Indian guy?"

"No. I talked with him a couple of times over the horn. I got the idea he was hot on a lead — but you know Mike . . ."

"You think he found something at the Public Record Office?"

"Nothing earth shaking. I talked with him about that. I know he was checking something out in Cambridge."

"He have a contact up there?"

"Yeah. A fellow named Snibley. He's a don at Trinity, I believe."

"OK," said Joseph, making a notation in his book, "I'll look him up."

"Swell! And keep up the good work!"

"I've only been here a day and a half. I ain't done nothing yet."

"If you need anything, just call."

"Send sun."

"Wish I could. Then I'd come over, too."

After he hung up, Joseph dialed a number.

She took a while to answer. Probably feeding the kid, Joseph guessed. When she finally came on the line he dispensed with formalities and just said, "What are we doing for dinner tonight?"

"I'm eating bangers and beans. How about you?" she replied.

"Gee — and I was just going to invite you to Claridges."

"Don't make me laugh."

"How about dessert?"

"I'm off sweets this week, luv."

"Coffee and a cigarette?"

She sighed. "Drop by after eight. I've still got a few things to do."

"See you then, Chuckles," he said.

He put the phone down and retrieved his bag from where he had left it on the stairs. After depositing it in the bedroom he went into the kitchen, filled the kettle with water and plugged it in. Unfortunately, the last tea-bag had been used and was sitting limply at the bottom of his banana cup. Making a face, he filled the cup with boiling water, gave the bag a stir and then gently lifted it out. There was a thin nail protruding from one of the cabinets. He stuck the corner of the tea-bag through and looked at it hanging there. Maybe it would dry and he could use it again. It couldn't taste any worse, he thought.

He took the warmish brew back into the living-room and sat down at his desk. He rubbed his eyes. "What am I doing here?" he heard himself say aloud. Then, looking down at the blue folder, still laying where he had left it that morning, he pulled out one of the pages at random. It was a photostat from the *Daily Telegraph*, Saturday, August 10, 1889:

"Conviction of mrs maybrick . . . Petitions from the northern circuit and liverpool merchants . . . The jury and their verdict . . . Our Liverpool correspondent telegraphed last night: 'The excitement caused by the Maybrick verdict has subsided a good deal today, but it cannot be said that the interest in the case is sensibly diminished. People have, as one gentleman remarked, their own business to attend to, and, though they are saying less about the case, there is no diminution in the feeling that the decision arrived at should be the subject of very careful review by the Home Secretary . . .'"

He let his eye scan down the page.

"We continue to receive correspondence from all parts of the country with reference to the verdict of the jury in the Maybrick case . . . To the editor: Sir — Thousands of men and women will want to know how and where they can add their names to a petition to the Crown to set aside this monstrous verdict in the Maybrick case. The horror with which the country has received the news that twelve men in thirty-five minutes condemned a woman to death when the case was so hedged round with difficulties that the judge took two days to sum up, is utterly without parallel . . . To the editor: Sir — I ask how, with the following facts before them, anyone could assert the absence of doubt? 1. That, among the medical witnesses, there was direct conflict whether arsenic was the cause of death. 2. It was established that the deceased was in the habit of taking arsenic on his own account. 3. It was alleged in medical evidence that, in the weak state of the stomach, gastro-enteritis might have been originated by some minor cause . . ."

He pulled out several more sheets — each photostats from newspapers. They all contained even more letters of outrage:

"To the editor: Sir — If Mrs Maybrick used infusion of fly-papers for a face-wash that would account for the traces of arsenic on her pocket-handkerchief, which she would certainly have to apply to her face at intervals, more or less frequent, during the day. The coincidence of arsenic being taken at the same time by the wife for external and by the husband for internal purposes is most unfortunate for Mrs Maybrick, but is no evidence against her . . . To the editor: Sir — Any wife who sees her husband suffering (even if she does not love him) would yield to his wishes and give him anything that would relieve his sufferings, especially when he had been in the habit of taking sundry drugs without any dangerous results. Certainly she had committed a great wrong in being unfaithful to her husband, but why should unfaithfulness in a wife be considered the most terrible sin she can commit and unfaithfulness in a husband considered nothing? If men bear in mind the marriage solemnization it is the same for men as women. Even if a woman is an adulteress, that is no reason why she should become a murderess. How the jury could have given the verdict guilty with so many doubts is beyond my comprehension. I earnestly hope that the miserable condemned woman will get a reprieve."

He put down the pages and thought a moment. Reaching for his notebook, he looked through some of the notations he had made from his readings on the Maybrick case. He leafed through the pages and then put it back down. It was all very unsatisfactory, he thought. Who was this woman, this Southern belle who ended up in a Liverpool jail? What actually happened on that fateful night? What was in the extract that she had given the maid to feed to her husband? Did it matter at all? And, even so, what the hell did it have to do with Lavinia Chancellor?

"Fuck it!" He threw his pencil across the room and watched it rebound off the wall. Then he got down on his hands and knees and, as much to relieve his anger as anything else, began pulling out all the desk drawers. He piled them one atop the other as he inspected them. They were empty, every one. He gave the pile a kick.

It was when he went to pick them up again that he saw it — an envelope neatly taped to the underside of the bottom drawer. He peeled it off and tore if open. Inside was a photograph. He inspected it closely. From what he could tell, it was a picture of an animal — from the looks of it, a goat — dangling stiffly from a miniature gallows, it's neck garroted in a hangman's noose.

He turned it over. On the back of the photo was scrawled the following words: "The Juwes are the men who will not be blamed for nothing."

Chapter 9

She wasn't covered in pudding this time when she came to the door. In fact, she looked rather nice. Her hair was combed and she was wearing a clean pair of slacks. Her blouse was one of those rayon kind that look silky to the touch. She even smiled as she told him to come inside. The fire was on. It was cozy and warm.

"Sean all tucked away to sleep?" he asked.

"One can always hope." She pointed to a tray on the table that had a Melitta pot over a candle fire. "Coffee waiting," she said. "It's fresh."

"Really? Fresh?" He looked slightly amazed.

"There's a shop by the Green that roasts it every day. That's their claim at least."

"You used a filter?" he asked.

"Of course."

"And you didn't pour the water in too fast?"

"One drop at a time."

He rubbed his hands together and went over to the pot. He glanced over at her before he picked it up. "May I?"

"Be my guest."

He poured a cup and handed it to her. She took it from him and smiled again. "Thanks."

"Two smiles in one night," he said, as he poured one for himself. "That must be some kind of a record."

"Don't blow it, Radkin," she said. She took a sip of her coffee and peered at him over the rim with her enormous eyes.

"Sorry . . ."

"Did you bring the cigarettes?"

He felt around in his jacket and came up with a pack. "Yeah." He pulled one out and tossed the pack over to her.

82

"What a gentleman," she said, watching the pack fall into her lap.

He lit his cigarette and tossed the matches. They landed on her lap next to the cigarettes. "If we don't want to play games then let's not," he said.

She stared at him a moment. "You're different to Mike . . ." she began.

"No kidding?"

"No kidding."

"How so?"

"He liked women."

"I like women, too."

"Not in the same way . . ." Taking one of the cigarettes from the pack, she lit up.

"Probably in the same way — in fantasy, that is. In reality, complications usually arise."

She puffed at her smoke. "And you've got a wife and kids."

"Yeah — about six thousand miles from here."

"Well, you get good marks for loyalty," she said.

"At least I get good marks for something," he replied, looking at her and wondering how he'd worked himself into the role of moralist. "Anyway, I thought I wasn't your type."

She crossed her legs and settled back in her chair. "You're quite cute in a rather pathetic way . . ."

"Maybe it's the dampness and the chill. It tends to bring out the pathetic in me. The cute I don't know about." He was beginning to feel slightly light-headed. "You have any sugar for this?" he asked.

"I thought you only put sugar in coffee to mask the taste. Don't you like it?" She sounded disappointed.

"It's great. I didn't eat, you see."

"What's wrong? Your wife not there to feed you? You do have a kitchen with a cooker."

He shrugged. "Forgot. The shops close so early."

"There's a Pakistani who stays open till ten around the corner."

"I don't like eating Pakistanis."

She got up. "I'll get some biscuits."

"Thanks," he said. Strange that he hadn't noticed before how attractive she was, he thought to himself, as he watched her go. He took a handkerchief from his pocket and wiped his brow.

She came back with a bowl full of sugar and something called "Rich Tea Biscuits" which turned out to be thin discs of sweetened cardboard, as far as he could tell. "Help yourself," she said.

He hadn't waited for the starter's orders. By the time she said it he had already begun to chew. "You have a magnifying glass?" he asked, stuffing another cookie in his mouth.

"You want to search for crumbs?" She looked at him in disbelief.

"I found something hidden in Mike's desk." He pulled out the photo. She came over and sat down beside him. There was a faint whiff of perfume as she reached over and took the photo from his hand.

"Looks like the window of a butcher shop," she said.

"Butchers use hooks, not ropes tied into hangmen's knots." He motioned for her to turn it over. "There's a curious message on the back."

"It is strange, I'll give you that," she said, glancing at the inscription.

She looked back up at him. Suddenly, he felt himself sinking into her eyes.

"Jesus, I forgot!" he said, nervously glancing at his watch. "I've got to make a call."

"I've got a telephone you can use," she replied.

He stood up. "I better use my own," he said, with a note of apology which sounded something like an out-of-tune piano. "It's to the States."

The wind was howling as he sallied forth across the street. Leaves, discarded newspapers, candy wrappers and the like blew past as he attempted to shield his eyes. He quickened his step. As he opened the door, the wind gusted into the hallway, leaving a raw chill on the unheated stairs. He climbed up to his rooms and turned on the lights. He thought of the graveyard he went to with Kate. At least there was life at the burial grounds. Here it was cold. Lonely and cold. Searching his pockets for some coins, he found only one. So it was either to be heat or light. Better not to switch on the heater, he thought. You could always wear a sweater, but you couldn't work in the dark — though, metaphorically speaking, working in the dark was exactly what he usually did.

He went to the window and drew back the lace. There was a glow coming from Kate's window. It was warm there. He sensed her fragrance even now. He let out a sigh, put his hands in his pockets and stood there for a moment, full of mixed emotions.

After a while, he went over to his desk and sat down. He opened up the folder and withdrew a page. It was an article dated Thursday, August 22, 1889:

"Our correspondent at Liverpool telephoned last night: On the announcement that the decision of the Home Secretary was likely to be made known today, much excitement was created in Liverpool, and constant inquiries were made at Walton Gaol, not only by those locally interested in the prisoner, but by people from a distance. Up to the time of dispatching this message no reprieve had reached the Governor of the gaol. In the forenoon a telegram was received from the Home Office, and shortly afterwards a reply was sent off to London by the Governor. This, however, had no reference to a reprieve, as shortly afterwards a telegraphic message arrived to the effect that Mr Addison, Q.C., the counsel for the prosecution, was having an interview with the Home Secretary. The telegram is believed to have had references to the condition of health in which Mrs Maybrick now is. This morning the Rev Mr Morris, chaplain to the gaol, visited Mrs Maybrick in her cell and conversed with her for some time on religious topics. She was also visited by the gaol doctor, who found her strength to be gradually getting less. There is no organic disease from which she suffers, but the anxiety and suspense have completely shattered her nervous system . . ."

There followed a letter: "To THE EDITOR: Sir — Kindly insert the following letter in your paper, and make the facts known as widely as possible, as I think they are important and will go far to prove Mrs Maybrick's innocence. In justice to her, though she is a perfect stranger to me, I wish to make these facts as public as possible. Some time ago I advertised that I ruled planets, cast horoscopes, etc., and thereby discovered intricate diseases incurable by medical man. I became known to and corresponded with many people; among others, with the late James Maybrick. He wrote me a strange account of his various ailments, and told me he was in the habit of taking large doses of arsenic and put some in his food, as he found that the best and safest way of taking it. He said it always aided his digestion and helped to calm his nerves when taken in that manner . . ."

Just then the telephone rang. The shock ran through his system like a jolt of electricity. He reached for the receiver: "Woof!" he barked into the mouthpiece.

"Joseph? Is that you?"

"Oh, Polly. Hi. I was just going to call you."

"Is there a dog living in your room?"

"No. Only me."

"I thought I heard a dog."

"That's because I feel like a dog — a cold, mangy, lonely and destitute pup."

"Poor Joseph. Why don't you come home. I miss you. The children miss you."

"Besides you and the kids, what's there to come back to? Polly, I need the work . . ."

"All right, I didn't call up to make a plea. It's just that you sounded so sad."

"I'll get over it as soon as I get something hot to eat and enough change to make a fire."

"Excuse me?"

"Never mind. How are you, Pol? Things going OK? No earthquakes in the last couple of days, I don't suppose."

"No earthquakes. How's the story going?"

"I've just been looking through some photostats that Mike had made from some old newspapers on the Maybrick case. There was sure a lot of interest in the press."

"There's always been interest in *femmes fatales*, especially if the *fatale* is arsenic, I suspect."

"All the papers, it seems, were besieged with letters, mostly from people who were outraged that she could be executed on so flimsy a case."

"Or executed at all, I would hope."

"You know, there must have been a pretty big anti-capital punishment movement building back then. Thousands of people flooded the Home Office with petitions."

"I wish they were around to do some of that now . . ."

"England got rid of capital punishment several years ago, Polly."

"I mean here. The blood is really beginning to flow."

"They're not hanging anybody, though."

"They might not be hanging them here but they're killing them right and left — gassing them, frying them, shooting them up with deadly poisons. I've been following this case down in Mississippi — a young black man convicted of rape and murder. The only substantial piece of evidence they had on him was a confession that he claims was extracted at the point of a gun. This kid is going to be gassed in Mississippi; that's the same state that used to hang young black men from apple trees. You were down there, Joseph. You tell me — you think a poor black kid, even today, can get a fair trial? You want a story? Come on home. You don't have to go to nineteenth-century England to find one!"

"The problem is, West is paying me to be here, not there. Anyway, the nineteenth-century bit is only half. There's the other case, Lavinia Chancellor. She's alive and in jail. I met her dad today. He's convinced she's innocent."

"He would be, wouldn't he? He's her father."

"Well you're convinced some kid in Mississippi is innocent and you haven't even met his dad."

"England's not Mississippi, though."

"It might not be as far from Mississippi as you think."

"Boy, you really must be feeling blue!"

"I suppose I am, Polly," he sighed. "I suppose I am. I'm beginning to feel like I've walked in on someone else's life."

"What?"

"Nothing. How are the kids?"

"Fine. They miss their daddy, though."

"Give them a kiss for me, Pol. And one for you, too."

They said their goodbyes and then he hung up. He rose from his chair and stretched. Looking down at his shoes, he saw they were scuffed. He rubbed a foot against the back of his leg and looked at the shoe again. It didn't help. In fact, he didn't really care. He felt something queasy in his stomach. Without really meaning to, he found himself walking over to the window again and pulling back the curtain. The wind was still blowing, scattering a trail of rubbish down the street. He put his nose closer to the glass and squinted his eyes. He thought he could see a figure standing at her door. It seemed to be a man. The door opened. He saw her standing in the doorway, but he couldn't see the other person's face. Then they went inside, shutting the door behind them. In a few minutes the lights in Kate's house went out.

Chapter 10

He heard a bird when he awoke the next morning. He didn't know where it was coming from; for all he knew, it could have been his head. The sleeping area was in a loft situated at the top of a narrow flight of stairs. Above the bed was a skylight without a shade. It meant you couldn't sleep too late without putting the covers over your eyes. He peeled them back and looked up and was amazed to see that the sky was colored a hazy shade of blue.

Swaddling himself in a blanket, he got out of bed, grabbed his toilet kit and went downstairs for a shower and a shave. There wasn't any shower, alas, so he stood in the tub and sponged himself down. Afterward, he was forced to look at himself in the mirror in order to shave. It was a scruffy visage that he saw, rather like his battered suitcase, and he didn't mind hiding it under a layer of shaving cream.

All this ritualistic cleansing, however, did give him a certain lift. Warm water and some soap often worked curious wonders on the mind. To Mrs White, cleanliness meant godliness. To him it meant a new beginning, like erasing the chalk marks on a blackboard or putting on a different disguise.

He rubbed down his face with some perfumed astringent that had a pleasant sting, like a friendly sort of slap — a masochistic relic from his straighter days when he worked for the daily press. Then he went back upstairs and put on some fresh clothes, punctuated by his one and only tie. Gazing at himself admiringly in a large mirror over the chest of drawers, he was about to concede that he looked almost debonair when he noticed a tuft of hair sprouting out of the back of his head. Each time he tried slicking it down, it would spring back. So much for vanity, he thought.

He was putting on his jacket when the telephone rang. He went to answer it.

"Radkin?"

"Yeah." He recognized the voice.

"Ron Chancellor here. How about a bite to eat?"

"Sure, I guess so. Could we meet somewhere near a tube stop? I need to go into town later."

"The West End?"

"The area where Virginia Woolf used to hang out."

"Are you familiar with Soho?"

"Did she hang out there, too?"

"Maybe under a different name. You know where it is, though?"

"Sort of, yeah."

"There's a small café called Mori's on Great Windmill Street, right by Piccadilly Circus. The museum isn't far from there. Just a ten-minute walk. Meet me in an hour."

Joseph usually liked sleazy areas. In most cities the places where professional sex was ghettoized had a certain kind of buzz. Rents were cheap, buildings were delapidated, so artists and bohemians coexisted out of need with the denizens of the night. But Soho had a different feel. It was as bleak as Orwell's *Nineteen Eighty-four*. It was sleaze all right, but it was sleaze without much soul.

Mori's was a small deli café that looked at first glance like it might have been in New York, but, in fact, turned out to be a wafer-thin imitation. Sure there was the necessary slab of salt beef laying like a half-eaten carcass on a smelly board with a hoard of groggy flies buzzing round the fat. But no upstanding New York deli would have displayed pickles that looked so limp and used, as if someone took a cucumber and left it in formaldehyde too long. And the bagels, which had been a sustaining force in his life back home, didn't even seem worth a nostalgic bite as he could tell even from a distance they were nothing more than a bread roll with a hole punched in the middle, instead of that wonderful mix of crust and dough which came to life through an intricate process of boil and bake — something Mori obviously didn't know.

Chancellor was seated alone at a table, reading the sports page of a tabloid paper. Joseph ordered coffee and a jam-filled doughnut and then went over to join him.

"You play the ponies, Sunshine?" he asked as Joseph sat down.

Joseph shook his head and then glanced at the doughnut. "Nah. I'd rather waste my money on stuff like this."

Chancellor took out a pen from his shirt pocket and circled something in red. He handed the paper over to Joseph and said, "If you have a tenner to spare and want a sure thing, try the third race, Newmarket."

Joseph glanced down at the listing. The horse was named Foxtrot. The owner was Palmerston. The jockey riding that day was Frank Carter. He looked up again. "Isn't Palmerston the name of the guy who's in the photo with your daughter and Fry?"

"There're lots of Palmerstons about," Chancellor replied.

"Newmarket's close to where Mike's body was found, right?"

"Not too far away."

"What do you think he was doing there?"

"Maybe he went there to bet on a race."

"He could do that just as easily from here," said Joseph motioning to the Littlewood's sign across the street.

"He could," said Chancellor. "But it wouldn't have been as much fun."

"What's fun about watching a bunch of horsemeat run in circles?" asked Joseph.

Ron took a sip of his tepid coffee and looked at him with eyes that were stone cold. "In Newmarket the field is straight. What do you do for kicks?"

Looking at the dingy surroundings, he said, "Sometimes, when I'm really hard up, I meet tired ex-cops in places like this." He reached into his jacket pocket and brought out an envelope which he handed to the older man across from him.

"Here's a present for you. I found it taped to the bottom of a drawer in Mike's desk."

The ex-cop opened the envelope and took out the photo Joseph had found. He squinted his eyes and set the photo down while he reached for his glasses. After putting them on, he inspected the photo again.

"There's something on the back," said Joseph.

Chancellor read the inscription on the other side.

"Mean anything to you?" Joseph asked.

He shook his head. Then he turned the photo over again and studied it.

"What do you think?"

"It was taken with a telephoto lens," said Chancellor.

"How do you know?"

"From the depth of focus and the shadows."

"Some kind of cult, perhaps?"

"I've seen cases of ritual slaughter," said Chancellor taking off his glasses and rubbing his eyes. "There's usually some sign of ceremony — symbols carved in the hide, viscera cut out, things like that." Looking at Joseph square in the face, he said, "You ever see an execution, Sunshine?"

Joseph shook his head.

"It's not a pretty sight. Not for squeamish eyes."

"Is it worse than the coffee here?" asked Joseph, taking out his pack of cigarettes. "You smoke?"

Chancellor shook his head. "Not anymore. Bad for the ticker."

He shrugged and lit up. "You got anything for me?"

Opening up a small satchel, Chancellor took out a folder. Inside was a document which he handed to Joseph. The letters running across the top said it was an autopsy report and it was Mike's.

"How'd you get it?" asked Joseph, glancing over the page and then looking back up at him.

"It fell into my hands."

"Is there something of interest I'm supposed to find? I guess you didn't give it to me for light entertainment."

"Did you ever read a report of a post-mortem examination before?"

"No. Not before breakfast anyway . . ."

"You only covered weddings in your newspaper career?"

"You don't have to read an autopsy report to know who, when, where and why," said Joseph defensively.

"It's how he died that matters," said Chancellor, with a note of disgust.

Joseph took the sheet and glanced through the report again. "As far as I can make out, there were massive internal injuries. That's enough to kill anyone."

"Read it again," said Chancellor. "There's less in what it answers than it asks."

"Like what?"

"Like curious marks and contusions. Like the way rigor mortis set in."

Joseph looked it over again and then handed it back. He inhaled a lungful of smoke and let it drift out of his mouth. "There's a lot you're not telling me, Ron."

"We'll take it slow," Chancellor said, sticking the paper back in his case. "I don't know how much I can trust you yet."

"Meanwhile your kid's in jail," said Joseph.

The muscles in Chancellor's face suddenly tensed. He leaned over and grabbed Joseph's shoulder and squeezed. "Listen," he hissed, "I could run around like a rooster with his goolies cut off, or I could do this right. If you want to help, that's up to you. But we'll do it my way, see?"

Chancellor's grip was like a vise. The pain shot through his arm like twenty tons of rusty spike.

Suddenly letting go of his shoulder. Chancellor sat back down. He took his cup and finished his coffee while Joseph rubbed his arm.

"I happen to know Fry was in pretty desperate straits before he died. He was always short of cash, but this time it was different. He needed some readies fast. Then suddenly something happened that made it all OK again."

"He struck oil, huh?"

"Yeah. And the oil was pretty black."

"Who?"

"Someone close to him."

"You have a name?" asked Joseph.

"Maybe I do," Chancellor said. He got up. "You searched your place thoroughly, Radkin?"

"I haven't torn the mattress apart if that's what you mean."

"Try the cupboards, the fridge, loose floorboards, things like that . . ."

"What am I looking for?"

"You'll know when you find it." He walked over to the door and then he turned around. "I'll telephone you soon. Maybe we can have a drink again."

"Yeah," Joseph replied, giving his arm another rub. "But next time you could leave your bone crusher behind."

The British Museum looked kinder today, basking in the semi-sun. The circus in the courtyard was in full swing devouring ice cream, drinks and lollipops. On the stairs, the troops had assembled, ready to pass in review before the relics of ancient lives. Joseph marched in behind and, instead of turning right, went straight on to present his letter of introduction to the guardians of all acquired human knowledge in printed form. In return they gave him a card with an instant photo pasted on. He looked at it and thought to himself that it was what they would call in the States a "shit-eating grin".

Shit-eating grin or not, it was this simple piece of plastic that allowed him to pass through the gates, into the sanctum-sanctimonious. But once inside, even his cynical demeanor seemed to melt. For here, underneath a classical rotunda that reached up to the sky, were concentric circles of people of all sizes and shapes, engrossed in the ancient art of study. And starting with the letter "A", going all around the room to "Z", were book after book of catalogues — simply that: catalogues which had the name and number of every book ever written in the language of English and quite a few others, besides. It was like looking up into the universe some cloudless night and counting all the stars. It tended to put one's work into some perspective.

After he regained his equanimity by recalling that entry here was supposed to be a privilege not a right, he went up to the information desk and took out his notebook. "I'm trying to find a book," he said, looking at the woman who was busily shuffling some paper behind the counter.

She handed him a form. "You'll find the information in the catalogues."

"All I have is the catalogue number, though," he said. "Is there a cross-reference?"

"You only have the catalogue number? Not the author or the title?"

"That's right," he smiled. "I just want to know what book it fits."

"Are you an American detective?" she asked.

"What if I told you I was a Chinese acrobat? Would it make any difference to you?"

"No. I was just wondering why anyone else would end up with only a catalogue number and want to know the title of the book."

"It is a mystery," he agreed. "But if you think about it, there are lots on intriguing mysteries in life — like dandruff, for example. Where does it go after it falls off our heads? I mean if the advertising agencies are correct, ninety percent of the human race is plagued with the stuff and with several billion people on earth, by rights there should be mounds of it all over the place as thick as Siberian snow. So where the hell does it go? Did you ever ask yourself that?"

She stared at him a moment. Then she answered, probably because to do otherwise would have been impolite: "No. I never asked myself that."

"So how do I go about it?"

She blinked her eyes. "What?"

"How do I go about finding out the author and title of the book?"

"Give me the number," she said, "I'll put it through. It might take a while, though."

"How long?"

"It depends. Maybe a day. Maybe two."

"How come?"

"There's no way to find out the author and the title without sending for the book. They're kept in depots around the city — that is, if they exist at all."

"What do you mean, 'if they exist'? It has a number, so why wouldn't it exist?"

She sighed. "Unlike America, we were bombed quite a bit during the war. Several thousand books were destroyed."

"I'm sorry," he said. "I hope they were given decent funerals." He realized it was the wrong thing to have said, even in jest.

"It's not a subject we find amusing," she snapped.

"Of course not," he said, trying on an apologetic grin. "It's just that I've noticed sometimes people get more upset about the fate of books, rhinoceruses and certain forms of algae than their fellow human critters."

"We at the British Museum find that one can be concerned with many things — even saving the rhinoceri — without excluding one's fellow critters."

"Then how come I needed a ticket to get in here?" he asked.

"We'd expect the same from a rhinocerus," she replied. "Come back in a few days. Maybe we'll have something for you. Maybe not."

Chapter 11

He went back to his room, ostensibly to work. But after a quick bite of some tasteless packaged cheese and a doughy thing the young man at the corner shop had called a "bap", he figured the best he could do was have a lie-down on the couch. Back in San Francisco, when he felt inclined to grab a quick afternoon snooze, he had always been obliged to give Polly an excuse — saying things like "Really, the subconscious plays an important part in any creative endeavour . . ." But Polly wasn't here, so he could lie there in peace, without guilt. Or so he thought. He hadn't closed his eyes for five minutes when the telephone rang. He let it ring a minute or so before he answered its persistent call: "Hello?"

"Mr Radkin?" It was a woman's voice — a high-class dame, from the sound of it.

"Yes. Who's this?"

"Virginia Hughes — Michael's mother. I wonder if we might have a little chat."

"Sure," said Joseph. "Chat away."

"Not over the phone, if you don't mind. Could you meet me for a drink this afternoon?"

"At your house?"

"No. I'd rather we met somewhere else . . ."

It was a marvelous old wooden building, painted snowdrop white and overlooking Hampstead Heath. She was seated at a table on the patio drinking tea when he arrived. There was a tray with service for two. She was wearing a wool suit that looked warm enough to withstand the chill and plenty of makeup to keep her skin from getting damp. A dead animal — maybe chinchilla, maybe fox — was flung around her neck.

97

She held out a jeweled hand as he came over and gave him the benefit of her charming smile.

"Thank you for joining me, Mr Radkin," she said as he took her manicured paw and gave it a shake. He didn't think he was supposed to kiss it. And if that was the idea, he thought, then she should have met him at a fancier café. "I took the liberty of ordering you some tea. I hope that's all right."

"Well, it's better than soda pop," he said as he sat down. "At least it's hot. What is it you wanted to talk to me about?"

"You're very direct, Mr Radkin, aren't you? As I recall, it's you who wished to talk with me."

She took a stainless-steel pot from the tray and poured some of its contents into an empty cup. "Do you take milk and sugar?" she asked, looking at him with her gorgeous eyes.

"Sure. Anything to hide the flavor of that stuff."

She put in a dollop of milk and a shovelful of sugar and handed him the cup. "You say you're taking Michael's place . . ."

"Only on the story he was writing," Joseph assured her.

"The one on the Victorian woman who was accused of murdering her husband with arsenic."

"Yes."

"Her name was Florence Maybrick, am I correct? She was American, I believe."

"Mike spoke to you about the case?"

"A bit. I found it interesting because it's something of my story in reverse. Not the murder, of course. Although when a vital man dies in his prime and leaves behind a young attractive wife there's always talk . . ."

"Mike's father, you mean?"

She nodded. "I met Michael's father some years ago when I traveled to America. I was just a girl. We had a whirlwind romance. He swept me off my feet and we married — but I was much too young to have known what it meant. I spent twenty-five years in Chicago, most of the time feeling like a prisoner in a very expensive jail."

"What did Mike's father do for a living?"

She hesitated a moment before she replied. "He was in the commodity trade."

"How about your present husband?"

"He's in the same business as my first."

"You know about the other case — the contemporary one?"

"Do you mean the Chancellor girl?"

"Did Mike speak to you about her?"

"Very briefly. Michael and I . . ." She let her voice drop.

He took a sip of tea and made a face. "When I came up to you at Mike's funeral, you said something about them taking him away. What did you mean?"

"Did I say that?" She shook her head. "If I did, I must have been referring to fate."

"Were you satisfied with Mike's autopsy?" he asked.

There was a slight tremor by the side of her mouth. "Why shouldn't I be?"

"Have you read the report?"

"The verdict was accidental death. That's all I need to know."

"There was some question of the injuries, I understand. Some of them didn't jibe with being run over by a truck. Marks on his wrist which could have been rope burns. Things like that . . ."

She looked at him in a way that made him sorry he had been so blunt. "Would questioning anything help bring my son back, Mr Radkin?"

"No," he replied. "But a couple of answers might help return someone's daughter."

There was a curious expression on her face as she stared into his eyes. "You know, just now you reminded me a little of nim," she said.

"Who?"

"My son."

"Mike and I don't look anything alike," said Joseph nervously.

"It's your manner more than your face," she said. And then

99

she sighed and took something from her purse. It was a calling card. "Towards the end he was searching for a man . . ."

"A man?"

She handed the card to Joseph.

"What's this all about?" he asked, looking even more puzzled.

She stood up and wrapped the fur around her throat. "I'm sorry, Mr Radkin," she said, "I've told you everything I can."

He watched her leave. She walked like a lynx. Very expensive property, he thought. Then he looked at the card. The name was Dr Singh. He turned the card over to see if there was anything written on it. But there wasn't.

He phoned the number on the card from a call box near the park. The recording which answered said Singh's phone was disconnected. Sticking the card into his wallet, he began walking back to his rooms.

As he walked, he tried mulling a few things over in his mind. The man Mike had been looking for, according to his mother, was most likely the man who was looking for Mike. But how did Virginia Hughes get a hold of the calling card? Was it in another one of Mike's shirts? And did this have anything to do with a hanging goat?

By the time Joseph reached Rona Road, he had decided to let it rest. The mystery of Dr Singh would have to wait until something else came his way.

He was feeling the pangs of either brain drainage or a severe sinus attack as he opened the front door of the White house. Looking down at his scuffed shoes, as he often did these days, he happened to see a letter addressed to "Mr Rose" laying on the floor. It had obviously been hand-delivered since there wasn't any stamp. He picked it up and put it in the pocket of his jacket.

When he got to his room he pulled the envelope back out. He opened it. It read: "Mr Rose: I got your note from Rasti at the Black Cat. Please! I'm just a working girl who needs to make her own way in the world. I have enough trouble as it is

— I don't need more! But I don't want to be responsible for some poor, unlucky woman spending her life inside Holloway neither. I know what that's like. It's hell! So if it helps, I'll tell you that about six months ago a bloke asked me to do a job — I never seen him before and I don't know his name. He spoke like a gentleman but maybe he was the filth. Anyway — all I was to do was wear a wig and go into King's pharmacy and ask for some strychnine to kill some rats. And for that I was given the sum of 100 quid — easier than making it lying on your back. I didn't ask no questions. Later I read about that poor Chancellor girl and I guess she was set up by someone for reasons I don't know. But — like I said — I have troubles of my own. If this information helps get an innocent woman out of jail, that's fine. Just don't get me involved. I sent a copy of this letter to both addresses you gave to Rasti. I hope you get it and can do something with the information. Now you can stop looking for me because that's all I got to say."

The letter was neatly typed and signed with just the initial "L".

As soon as he read it, Joseph took out his notebook, grabbed the phone and dialed the number he had down for Ron Chancellor. He let the phone ring while he lit up a smoke. No one answered.

"Fucking cops!" he shouted, slamming down the receiver. "Never there when you need them!"

He picked up the phone again and dialed Kate's number. He dragged the contraption over to the window and pulled back the curtain as he listened to the ring. Nothing stirred across the road — not as far as he could see.

He slammed the receiver down once more and searched his notebook for another number. He found it and dialed.

Beatrice Kendal wasn't in. "She never is," said her secretary. "I keep trying to have her get one of those modular telephones, but frankly I think she'd just leave it somewhere along with her mittens and her coat."

"It's a matter of life and death!" Joseph shouted. "I've got to get in touch with her at once!"

"It's always a matter of life and death, isn't it? I mean what other options are there?"

"Listen to me!" Joseph hollered, waving the letter in the air. "I have in my hand some evidence that could free one of her clients!"

"Well," said the voice, "I know she'd be delighted to hear it. You'll be very careful with it — whatever it is you have — won't you?"

"Can I get in touch with her today or not?" he said in a voice oozing with frustration.

"That really depends . . ."

"Depends? Depends on what?"

"It depends on whether you can make it to the Swiss Cottage Neighbourhood Centre in the next ten minutes. She's giving a talk there on child prostitution. Do you know how many fourteen-year-olds are selling their bodies on London streets? It's truly shocking!"

"Yes, yes," said Joseph. "My heart bleeds. Where did you say she was again?"

"Swiss Cottage. She'll be finished with question time and just about to call a taxi now, unless I miss my guess . . ."

He flagged down a cab at the Gospel Oak station. It took about fifteen minutes for the hack to make it across town to Swiss Cottage. When they reached the community-center complex Joseph flipped the driver a fiver and barged out the door. He hopped across the road and ran straight up to another cab idling by the curb. Beatrice Kendal was just getting in.

"Hi!" he said. "Can I ride along with you?"

She stared at him over the tops of her ivory-frame glasses. "You're not an encyclopedia salesman are you? Because if you are, I must tell you I'm absolutely aghast at the new *Britannica* . . ."

He shook his head. "I'm a journalist. I interviewed you the other day, remember?"

A look of recognition suddenly came over her face. "Oh

yes, of course. You're the American chap doing the story on the Chancellor girl."

He smiled. "And I've got a little something for you." With a flourish that had a trace of smugness, he handed her the letter.

"What's this?" she asked, looking at him quizzically.

"You'll see," he said, giving her a little wink.

She glanced down at her watch. "You'd better come along with me," she said, getting into the cab. "I'm on a very tight schedule today."

As the taxi drove off she unfolded the letter and scanned the contents.

"Ah, the famous 'L' note," she said. "Or should I say infamous."

He couldn't hide his surprise. "You mean you've seen it before?"

"I really hate to disappoint you, Mr Radkin — you look so like a boy whose balloon has flown away — but, yes, I must admit I have," she said, refolding the letter and handing it back to him. "It's got around almost as much as you, my dear chap."

"But have you read it? It seems to me it's a signed affidavit that refutes the only damning piece of evidence used to convict Lavinia Chancellor!"

She shook her snow-white head. "Wrong on all counts, I fear, Mr Radkin. Firstly, it's not an affidavit, but merely a note. Secondly, it's not signed but initialed. Thirdly, it's not written in anyone's hand — that is to say, it's typed. And fourthly, there's no witness to the name — nor, indeed, is there a name at all."

Joseph closed his eyes. "So you're not even going to investigate it?"

"Did I say that? Goodness me!"

He opened his eyes again and looked at her. "Then you are?"

"We already have, dear boy . . ."

"And?"

"Your Mr Rasti has been convicted of dealing in substances considered to be harmful to one's health. He, therefore, as far as the law is concerned, is not the most credible witness even if

103

he were willing to testify that he handed a note from your colleague to a certain woman."

"But what about the woman?"

"There was a woman — an acquaintance of Mr Rasti's. A Miss Lulu, as I recall . . ."

Joseph waved his hand in the air as a sign of his frustration. "And?"

"I'm afraid she's dead, Mr Radkin."

"What?" He acted as if he didn't hear.

"I said, 'I'm afraid she's dead.'"

"How long?"

"It's been several weeks now."

"What was the cause of death?"

"She was fished out of the Thames. I don't know whether you've had an opportunity to view our nation's waterways, but several hundred years of industrial sewage has taken its toll. A few days' soak makes it rather difficult to do a serious pathological report. And when the victim is — how shall I say? — a woman of the night . . ." She shrugged her shoulders.

"But surely there's enough evidence here to have a review of the trial."

"What we have, Mr Radkin, is a series of circumstances which you have chosen to interpret in a certain way. We have a note, a dead woman, and a man who will not talk."

"And the note says Lavinia Chancellor is innocent!"

"I could type another one saying she was guilty and send it to you in a similar manner." She narrowed her eyes. "How did you receive this letter, might I ask?"

"Underneath my door. It was sent to my colleague. I don't know who sent it to him."

"Whoever did is slightly behind the times, I'd say."

"I was given something else today that might have a bearing on the case." Joseph pulled out his wallet and took out the calling card. He showed it to her. "Do you know anything about this Dr Singh?"

"I've never heard of the man," she said.

"It was given to me by my colleague's mother. She said Mike was looking for him."

"Ah. The formidable Mrs Hughes."

"You know her?" Joseph asked.

"I know of her, Mr Radkin . . . through the doings of her present husband, of course."

"Cecil Hughes . . ." Joseph let the sound run over his tongue and decided he didn't like the taste. "What do you know about him?" he asked.

"One knows rather little of the rich and powerful — except the silly things the papers say. And that's hardly worth a mention."

Despite himself, Joseph found he took offense. "The papers sometimes give a few insights. Not too often, I grant you that."

"Ah, yes. I'd almost forgotten. You're a journalist yourself."

"I try not to write too many silly things — at least not in the same paragraph." He lit up a cigarette and looked at her. "You mind if I smoke?"

"If you insist," she said, rolling down the window on her side of the cab. "I might have been a little overzealous in my condemnation of the fourth estate. The press, at its best, can give us some valuable information — if we're astute enough to read between the lines."

"And what have you surmised from those blank spaces between the print regarding Cecil Hughes?"

"What one can glean about Mr Hughes isn't very nice."

"For instance?"

"Think of a giant octopus, Mr Radkin. Then picture Hughes Industries as its head and the tentacles its component parts — shipping, insurance, factories, farms. Now envisage each tentacle around the throat of another smaller octopus . . ."

"Big fish always eat the small," said Joseph, letting a trail of smoke stream from his mouth. "It's the way of the world."

"There is a difference between eating and bludgeoning to death. I don't wish to engage you in theories of economics. However, I would remind you of an atrocity that was reported in the papers less than a year ago, involving a ferry carrying several thousand Muslim pilgrims which sank in stormy seas. Hundreds of hapless victims were trapped below deck without a chance of escape. Hundreds more were without life-preservers."

"Yeah, I remember reading about it — a real tragedy."

"It was more than a tragedy, Mr Radkin, it was a crime of the highest magnitude. One that will never reach a criminal court — alas."

"Did Hughes have anything to do with that?"

"Very much so — yes. The tentacles of the octopus reach far and wide — half-way across the globe, if need be. When safety regulations somewhere hamper their profits, they simply reach out somewhere else. Just as with that chemical plant which exploded killing scores of people and making thousands of acres uninhabitable for generations to come. The same type of factory was shut down for safety reasons here. They just opened it again in a thirstier part of the world — under a different name, of course."

"Hughes Industries again?"

"Through a complicated network of paper corporations."

"There're lots of civil suits coming out of that gaff. Hopefully it'll be enough to bankrupt them."

"Not when you have controlling interest in insurance companies. An octopus is an unusual creature. When you cut off a tentacle another one always grows in its place."

Joseph thought back to the meeting he had with Mike's mother that morning. "Mrs Hughes told me her husband was in the commodities trade."

"I wouldn't dispute it," Beatrice Kendal replied. "After all, what are the world's most expendable commodities, Mr Radkin?"

"You tell me."

"People," she said simply.

The cab pulled over to the side of the road. Beatrice Kendal reached for her purse and took some money out.

"Where are we?" Joseph asked, gazing through the window

at a dour-looking building which seemed nearly as grey as the sky.

"Victoria Hall. I'm addressing a meeting of the Anti-Vivisection League tonight."

Chapter 12

Heading back to Gospel Oak the sky began to darken filling the space where gloomy greyness once had been.

"We're in for a bit of weather, guv," said the cabby as he swung his Austin into Rona Road.

"What do you call the stuff we had before?" asked Joseph as he handed the driver a ten-pound note.

"Nothing compared with what's coming now," the cabby replied.

Joseph had just enough time to collect his change before the sky opened up. By the time he made it inside, he was soaked from head to foot. The dripping water from his clothes left a trail on Mrs White's fluffed-up carpet like a puddle from a dog with a bad kidney. He let out a sneeze. Pneumonia weather, he thought to himself, as he took off his shoes and socks and then his shirt. He listened for the sound of cleaning machines, and hearing none, he figured it was safe to undo his belt and pull his trousers off too.

Wrapping his clothes into a soggy bundle, he started walking down the hall. The darkness from the storm had made it hard to see. He tried the switch at the bottom of the stair-well, but the light on the staircase wouldn't turn on.

Blown fuse, he told himself as he felt his way up the steps. He remembered afterwards sensing something wasn't right. Perhaps it was the aura of the storm. He heard a noise and thought it was a rat. A small rat, of course. More like a mouse. He hadn't expected anything so big as he opened the door to his room and walked inside.

It had the force of a small explosion. He felt it on the back of his head. There was a maddening roar in his ears and then a rush of blood. And that's all he remembered before he collapsed.

His ears were still ringing when he opened his eyes. He sat up and shook his head. He rubbed the spot where a tuft of his hair stood on end. There was an enormous bump.

Replaying the scene in his mind, he realized that whoever had been waiting for him must have heard him going up the stairs. He noticed a chair had been placed by the door, flush against the wall. Maybe the rat had been sitting there.

The room was a mess. The desk drawers had been removed. The couch was overturned. The carpet had been pulled up. Mrs White would not be pleased, he thought.

He went into the kitchen and let the water run. He splashed some over his face. A window by the sink led to the air vent. It had been opened and he wondered whether the intruder could have used the sewage pipes that ran down the side as a way up.

He boiled some water and took the dried-out tea-bag from its hook. He made himself a cup of something stale and hot. Then he lit up a cigarette and had a smoke. It made him feel better, but not much.

Still a little shaky on his feet, he returned to the scene of the crime. He put the drawers back in the desk and righted the couch. As he bent to straighten the carpet, however, he noticed that one of the floorboards had been marked in such a way that led him to suspect it had once been pried up. He reached in his pocket for his knife, kneeled down and puttered with it round the edges of the plank. The nails were loose and the wood came up without difficulty. Reaching down into the hole he had exposed, he felt around with his hand. Within the dark crevice among the cobwebs and the dust he discovered something that felt like paper. He pulled it out. It was an envelope.

Carefully he tore it open and inspected the contents. Inside there was a tiny strip of negatives. He took out the strip and was holding it up to the light when the telephone rang. He went over to the desk and picked it up.

"Radkin?"

"Yeah. What's left of him."

"What are you doing for dinner?"

"Actually, Kate, I've got a bloody awful headache . . ."

"I made some cannelloni."

"Fresh?"

"Yes. And Sean popped off to sleep . . ."

"I'll be right over," he said.

The rain had abated when Joseph made his way across the road. He saw her standing at the window, waiting for him. He hardly had time to knock at the door before she opened it.

"Hello," she said with a nervous smile. "Come in."

He nodded and walked inside.

"How's your head?" she asked, taking his jacket from him and hanging it on a hook.

"My head?"

"'Bloody awful headache,' you said on the phone . . ."

"Oh . . ." He felt the bump. "Better. Had a little accident," he said.

"What happened?" she asked, taking some plates from the sideboard and bringing them to the coffee-table.

"I bumped into a cosh," he replied, watching her closely and noticing that she avoided his eyes.

"You have to be more careful."

He sat down on the couch. "It's hard to plan for people who wait for you behind closed doors."

She came over to where he was and walked to the other side of the couch. He couldn't see her, but he felt the warmth of her hand on the back of his head. "It's not a pretty cut," she said.

"I've never seen a pretty cut," he said. "Have you?"

She left the room and came back a few moments later with a pan of water, a cloth and some soap.

"You got a license to do this?" he asked, as she began to wash the bruise.

"I'm a mum," she said. "Mums spend half their life doing things like this."

"What about the other half?"

"The other half they spend warning kids to keep out of mischief."

"If there wasn't any mischief, I'd be out of work."

"Perhaps you should find yourself another job," she said.

"Maybe it's too late," he replied.

She put down her cloth. "All done," she said. "I'm afraid you'll live." She collected her equipment and took it back into the other room.

"How about you?" he called after her.

"How about me?"

"You seem to live pretty dangerously, too."

She came back carrying a casserole full of steaming food. "The difference," she said, placing the dish down on a hotplate, "is that I can take care of myself."

"Think you're pretty tough, do you?" he asked her.

"Tough enough," she replied, spooning some tomatoey stuff into his plate.

He took the plate and held it up over his head. He gave her a little smile and then he dumped the contents on the floor. The tomatoey stuff oozed slowly into the rug.

"What did you do that for?" she said, looking at him aghast.

"Just to see how tough you really were," he replied, getting up and walking toward the door.

"Bastard!" she called out.

He grabbed his jacket from the hook. Then he turned around and said, "At least when I do something to someone, I do it in front of them, Kate."

He called McIssacs from a phone box near his house.

"Hi," he said. "You in the mood for visitors?"

"From outer space?" McIssacs asked.

"From beyond the grave," said Joseph.

The small Victorian house was situated on a tree-lined street in Kilburn just a short distance from Gospel Oak on the

Richmond rail line. Joseph could hear the powerful voice of an Italian diva singing an aria from *The Barber of Seville* when he knocked at the door. So, he supposed, could all the neighbors.

McIssacs handed him a glass of Chianti as he came inside. He was wearing an apron thick with spots of yellow crust.

"I've been trying my hand at polenta," he said, ushering Joseph into the cozy front-room, "but all I seem to get is lumps."

"Polenta isn't easy," Joseph replied. "It's best made in a cast-iron pan."

"And eaten by someone with a cast-iron stomach, I suppose," McIssacs said, tossing aside a copy of Gramsci to make room for Joseph to sit down. "Maybe I should face it. I just can't do Italian."

"You could always try learning Russian," Joseph suggested.

McIssacs shook his head. "Caviar's much too expensive and vodka goes to my head. Besides, Russian ladies are too fat."

Joseph looked around. "You live here alone?" he asked.

"I do now," McIssacs replied.

"She didn't like your cooking? Or did she run off with the lead singer in a heavy-metal band."

"She's in India learning Tantra from a bald-headed man who wears an orange mackintosh."

"Anyone who'd do that isn't worth shedding too many tears about."

"I know." McIssacs licked the top of the spatula he still carried in his hand. "But she could make the best calzone you'd ever want to eat. Calzone that would make the angels sing."

He let out the briefest of sighs. Then grabbing a Stetson from a pile of hats sitting on a nearby table, he put it on his head, thrust his thumbs in his pockets, looked Joseph in the eye and, in a near-perfect Western accent, said, "So what brings you to this part of town, buckaroo? Wild Bill and his gang of desperados passed this way about an hour ago. They tied up little Jennie Lee and made off with her ma. They shot up the dance hall and handcuffed the sheriff to his hoss and then took off. They're probably half-way to Mexico by now . . ."

Joseph took the envelope from his jacket pocket and pulled out the tiny strip of film. "You have a projector or something we can use to view this?"

"Let's see," said McIssacs in a more serious tone of voice. He held the strip Joseph handed him up to the light. "Microfilm. Where'd you find it?"

"Let's say it found me."

"I don't have any proper equipment," said McIssacs, motioning for Joseph to follow him, "but maybe we can dig something up."

McIssacs led the way into the adjoining room which appeared to be his study. A desk set off to one side was strewn with newspaper and magazine cuttings. From underneath the desk, McIssacs withdrew a large cardboard box and began rummaging around. After pulling out a few odds and ends, he came up with a magnifying glass — the kind elderly people use to read small print. Then, adjusting his desk lamp so it was directed toward the wall, he looked at Joseph and said, "Let's have that strip of film again."

Joseph handed him the tiny negatives. McIssacs tried to project an image on the wall by holding the strip between the light and the magnifying glass, but to no avail. "The light's too diffuse," he said. "We need to focus it."

He rummaged through the carton again until he came up with some stiff black paper which he then used to construct a box. In one end he inserted the lamp; in the other he made a small hole.

"Now," he said to Joseph, "turn out the lights and then come over here and hold the strip of film."

As Joseph held the film, McIssacs played around with the lens until they got the proper distance to project against the wall. It was still slightly blurred, but they could see.

113

The first frame was the picture of the hanging goat — the print of which Joseph had found taped to the underside of a drawer in Mike's desk.

"Strange what people do for laughs," said McIssacs.

"I've seen it before," said Joseph, moving on to the next frame of the film. Bringing the image into focus, they saw what appeared to be the exterior of a manor house. The frame after that was of the same house, but a closer shot. With a small adjustment of the lens they could make out the name above the door.

"Foxton Manor," Joseph read. "Ever hear of it?"

"No."

The fourth frame seemed to be a membership list. "Some sort of Masonic group, judging from the graphic symbols," said McIssacs.

"'James Berry Memorial Lodge'. You know who this Berry guy was?"

"The name rings a bell," said McIssacs. "Let me have a think."

The list of names was printed in type too small to decipher. So they went on to the last frame which contained a shot of a document, a purchase order from a pest control company, made out to Foxton Farms, for ten liters of pesticide trademarked "Strykill".

"What do you think?" asked Joseph when they turned the lights back on.

McIssacs glanced at his watch. "Too late to check the university reference library tonight." He went over to some thick volumes resting on a shelf. "Let's see if that Berry chap is listed in any of my biographies."

They went through a pile of old *Who's Who*s before giving up.

"I guess he wasn't that well known," said Joseph.

"Or possibly in some profession not deemed worthy of mention."

"How about Foxton Manor? Can we look that up?"

"Perhaps in a guide to stately homes."

"You got one of those about?" asked Joseph, looking at the array of elderly books decomposing on the shelves.

McIssacs shook his head. "I should have done. You never know when you might need it, do you?"

"How about the pesticide? You have something that could help us there?"

"I've got a pharmacopoeia. But what's written on the purchase order is a trade name. Besides, pesticides wouldn't be listed."

Joseph shrugged. "So I guess we struck out."

"For the moment," said McIssacs. "We just need a few hours access to a decent research library, that's all." He stopped and then said, "Care to tell me what this is all about?"

"Maybe later," said Joseph.

"Maybe later," McIssacs repeated. "The story of my life."

"I'm sorry," said Joseph. "It's just that when I'm doing an investigation I find it better . . ."

McIssacs held up a hand. "You needn't explain. I know about you chaps who lead secret lives . . ." He made his finger into a gun and squinted an eye. "Ducking bullets . . ." He wiggled his eyebrows. "Seducing *femmes fatales* . . ." He waved a hand at his cluttered bookshelves. "And what do I have? Dust and boredom."

"You could always join the Foreign Legion," said Joseph.

"Don't think I haven't considered that," McIssacs said, looking through the window into the darkness. "*Mamma mia!* It's started to rain again." He looked back at Joseph. "There's plenty of room here if you would care to spend the night."

"Thanks," said Joseph. "Maybe I'll take you up on that."

"Fine," said McIssacs, with a cheery smile. "I'll bring out the grappa!"

The "grappa" turned out to be a bottle of decent Scotch. They were in the front-room by the fire, watching the flames devour the remains of an old pine chair that had been turned

115

into kindling, and half-way through the bottle when McIssacs turned to him and said, "What do you know about Baroness Von Roques?"

"Nothing. Who is she?" asked Joseph.

"Florence Maybrick's mother."

"I thought her maiden name was Chandler," said Joseph, looking at him quizzically.

"It was. But her mother's first husband died. Some years later she married a Prussian cavalry officer. In between she was betrothed to a young confederate naval captain. He died a year after their marriage. There were rumors, of course . . ."

"What kind of rumors?"

"A waft of bitter almonds. No formal charges were ever brought against her. But like her daughter she was a stranger in a closed society. A Yankee marrying a Southern officer during the time of the Civil War. You can imagine what they thought of her down there in the land of mint juleps and pecan pie."

Joseph stuck a poker in the smouldering fire and watched the sparks shoot up with the draft. "Still, it's like ghosts from the past, isn't it? A mother suspected of the very crime her daughter gets convicted for."

"She was an interesting old girl."

"Von Roques?"

"Yes. Came from a long line of aristocratic thieves. Her father was Darius Halbrook, you know."

"No. I didn't know. Who's he?"

"He was a land speculator. One of the founders of Cairo, Illinois, in fact. Somehow he got some very prestigious English bankers interested in his land deals — people who thought they'd make a killing in the American land boom. Famous names, too, like Charles Dickens. Actually, what he set up was a house of cards. And when it collapsed it touched off something of a financial panic on both sides of the Atlantic. The scandal created quite a stink for many years."

"Seems hard to believe it could have had a bearing on the Maybrick case though," said Joseph, throwing another bit of chair onto the fire.

116

"Perhaps," McIssacs said, "but the curious thing about the British upper-class is the smallness of the circle. It's very ingrown. Everyone knows everyone else."

"Not like now, huh?"

"Oh, I wouldn't say that," McIssacs replied, taking a final drink. "When you get really up into the social stratosphere, the circle is very, very tight."

"How about a man like Cecil Hughes," asked Joseph. "Would he be likely to know someone like Reginald Palmerston?"

"You mean Hughes of Hughes Industries and Palmerston, the son of the High Court judge? You bet your sweet bottom! At this very moment, the two of them are probably sitting at the Tory Club in front of an oak fire — no need to hack up chairs in their part of the woods — drinking a far better whisky than we are now."

Joseph held his glass up to the light, admiring the amber texture. "This stuff's not so bad," he said.

"Strange you should mention Palmerston, though," said McIssacs, rubbing his chin.

"Why's that?"

McIssacs looked at him in a curious way. "Because it was his family's bank I was talking about — the one that went bust in the Halbrook scandal."

Chapter 13

He awoke with a start. A hazy ray of light came through the dirty window cutting a smoky path through the disheveled room. He felt a throbbing in his head as he sat up and rubbed his eyes, trying to orient himself once more, searching for a little map tucked somewhere in his brain that could help locate him within the vastness of space.

The couch he had been sleeping on was surely next in line to be hacked up for the fire, he thought, as he rubbed his aching back. It fit perfectly the Protestant notion of comfort as a form of sin. Luther himself could have designed it. Either him or a committee from the Inquisition.

An empty whisky bottle sat on the table at the spot where the wilted flowers had once been. Underneath it was a note made out to him. It was written on a huge piece of paper with red ink, so he could hardly miss it.

"Radkin: Your snoring woke the cat. But you were sound asleep — heaven knows how with all that din! I have a morning class but I'll pop into the library around noon and see what I can dig up there. You can phone me at my office later. Give the door a slam when you leave. Ciao, McIssacs."

He made himself some coffee in McIssacs' Italian espresso pot. There wasn't much in the larder. Just some stale bread and jam. He made himself some toast. Then, pulling Mike's diary from his jacket pocket, he sat down, had his simple breakfast, and pondered a notation he had thought about before. The entry Mike had made was "East End Books. Whitechapel". And after that, underlined in red, was the name: "Lipski".

He had run across that name in the leading article on the Maybrick case he had been reading the other day. It was a simple line: "The warning given by Lipski's case should not be forgotten . . ." He had gone through the article twice again; there was no hint as to who Lipski was or what his case was all about, except the sentence which preceded it: "We are very sensible of the inadvisability of retrying by the Press a case which has been decided after much careful consideration by a competent jury." And that was all that was said. But clearly, Joseph thought, this fellow Lipski had caused enough of a stir in his time for them to have used him as a warning, without the need to remind the reader who he was and what he did that was important enough for the press to have retried him at all.

East End Books was just off Whitechapel High Street, near the Aldgate tube. To get there you had to go through a narrow alleyway that ran between a gussied-up gallery and a dark brick structure which looked and smelled as if it hadn't changed that much since Dickens' day. A bold sign painted on the wall by someone who was schooled in serious graffiti indicated the bookshop was down the passage. If this were New York or San Francisco, he would have been more hesitant about strolling down an alley like this all alone. But here grime didn't necessarily spell danger. It might have been just something left over from Dickens, that was all.

The graffiti-painter's arrows led him round a bend and through a door into a subterranean print-shop. Inside, a dark spray hung in the air like thick, black mist. A worker, oiling an overheated press, wiped his inky brow and looked at him.

"East End Books?" Joseph shouted through the din. The clatter of the press was too much for anyone to speak and to be heard. But a few months in that noisy dungeon and you learn to lip-read, Joseph thought. The worker pointed up and Joseph ascended a narrow flight of stairs.

At the top of the landing were two doorways, one to the right and one to the left. The one to the right was open; the other one was closed. He stood by the open one and looked in. There were so many volumes stuffed into the tiny room, crammed in bookshelves and stacked on tables and even

119

chairs, that he wondered how they fitted a customer inside. Not that it seemed a problem though; not today, anyhow, for the place was empty — at least of breathing life.

He was mulling over his next move, when he heard the door open at his back. The voice was a mixture of friendliness and suspicion. "Can I help you find something?"

Turning around, he saw a man who wore a thickly bearded smile and a sparkle in his eyes. "It seems to me you'd need a bloodhound with a bulldozer to find anything in there," Joseph said.

"It might look a mess," said the beard, "but I know where everything is and I'll find it ten times faster than your ordinary bookshop."

"That's because your ordinary bookshop has probably sent it back to the publisher," Joseph replied as he squeezed himself inside. He lifted a book from the table and brushed off the dust. "Is there much call for Bukharin's speeches from the Plenary Session of the 1920 Party Congress anymore?"

"You'd be surprised," said the beard. "Bukharin's back in favor now. This time next month we probably won't have a single copy left. So if you want it, you better get it while you can."

"I'll keep it in mind," said Joseph, putting the book down.

The beard smiled again and stuck out his hand. "They call me 'the Digger'," he said. "Can I get you anything — coffee, tea . . . ?"

He shook the guy's hand. "Radkin. Joseph Radkin," he said. "This place double as a café, too?"

"No. You obviously don't want a book, though. I should think you want to talk . . ."

Joseph let out a chuckle. "Sure."

"What'll it be then? Coffee? Most Americans like coffee . . ."

"What kind?"

"Pure Nicaraguan."

"Sounds better than a bat on the head."

120

"Politically, yes. But if you really want the truth, I prefer the more reactionary stuff from Colombia," he said as he left.

Joseph was glancing through a book of photos on the East End a hundred years ago when the Digger came back into the room carrying two steaming mugs, one of which read "Dare To Struggle" and the other, "Dare To Win". He handed "Dare To Struggle" to Joseph.

"So what's this all about?" the Digger asked.

Joseph took a sip of coffee and thought it wasn't bad. "I found the name of your shop in the diary of a friend. I think he might have come here for some information."

"Lots of people come here for information. Knowledge is power . . ."

"Except this guy's dead."

The smile faded from his face. "Was your friend also American?"

"Yeah. A journalist from Frisco. Name of Rose. Mike Rose. Ring a bell?"

The Digger stroked his beard. "He came to talk to me about the Lipski case." And then, looking into Joseph's eyes, he said, "As, I suppose, you did too."

The wind swept down Whitechapel High Street toward the mosque, following the direction of the star and crescent.

"This area used to be like the East Side of New York," said the Digger as they walked. "In the 1880s the streets were packed with bearded men dressed in long black overcoats and women with babushkas tied around their heads. They all spoke Yiddish. Most of them were dirt poor. They left Poland and Russia without a penny and came here expecting the streets to be paved with gold. After all, this was the richest country in the world back then. What they didn't know was that the wealth was all in the hands of the upper classes. And there was hardly any work. So, in order to survive, they jungled up twenty to a room. When Engles did his study on English poverty, this is the area he focused on."

"He could have come to the States. It was pretty much the same back then."

"I'm sure you're right," the Digger said. "It just depended on what ship you got on. You could have ended up in London, Glasgow, Buenos Aires or New York. You never really knew until you hit the shore."

"Yeah, well there's a new wave sweeping the streets today," said Joseph, noticing the mix of costumes and colors that passed by.

"Nearly as vulnerable, if not as poor."

They had turned down Commercial Road now, heading east. "About the Lipski case . . ." Joseph began.

"It's one of those cases still shrouded in mystery," said the Digger, "but I'll tell you what I know. In 1887, the summer of Victoria's Golden Jubilee, a young umbrella-stick maker by the name of Israel Lipski was accused of killing a woman who lived in the same house. It was a particularly brutal case. The woman — Miriam Angel — lived right below Lipski's workshop, which was in the attic of a small house on Batty Street, in the heart of the Jewish East End. She was some months' pregnant. Lipski was accused of raping her and forcing nitric acid down her throat."

"Nitric acid?" Joseph repeated, feeling the stale toast and marmalade from the morning churning inside his stomach. "He didn't use it to get high, did he?"

"Not likely. It was an ingredient used in the staining process by stick-makers back then."

Joseph scratched his head. "So what is there about it that interested Mike so much? Sounds like a typical case of murder most foul to me."

"There were several curiosities in the case," the Digger continued. "First, Lipski, himself, was found poisoned and unconscious underneath Miriam Angel's bed. The story he told, in Yiddish, of course, was that two men who he had hired to help him in his attic workshop had actually done the deed. Lipski claims he found them in the process of robbing the room, after they had disposed of the woman, when he

122

returned with some supplies. The two men grabbed Lipski and forced acid down his throat — as they had done to her — and then dumped him underneath her bed."

"Why wasn't he believed?" asked Joseph.

"Because when Miriam Angel's body was discovered and Lipski was found underneath her bed, the door to the room was locked — locked, I should add, from the inside."

Joseph rubbed the wound on the back of his head and thought a moment. "That does sound somewhat incriminating," he agreed.

"Not really," said the Digger. "The defense was able to get expert testimony saying that it would have been quite easy for anyone with the slightest knowledge of locks to have turned the key, which had been inserted in the lock on the inside of the door, from the outside. There was a special tool for it that most locksmiths — and robbers —kept in their kits."

"Was there any other evidence against Lipski?"

"None that came out during the trial. He seemed to be a rather nice young man. No one really had a bad word to say about him. He was a typical immigrant Jew who had come from Poland about six months before. Lipski had worked for an umbrella-maker — he was engaged to the man's sister-in-law, in fact — and had just set up his own stick-making shop. He hadn't any money, but neither did Miriam Angel. And his future certainly seemed a great deal brighter than many other immigrants, who shared his lot and didn't feel the need to resort to murder."

"OK," said Joseph. "So maybe he was innocent and maybe he wasn't. I still don't understand what made the case so important."

"What made the case so important was the press. There was a newspaper in those days — the *Pall Mall Gazette*. Ever heard of it?"

"Yeah, I read a few issues concerning the Maybrick case."

"The *Gazette*, in fact, was a test tube for the ideas of a man named W. T. Stead — a fascinating bloke. Died on the *Titanic*, I believe. Stead took an interest in the case. Partly because of the uniquely morbid nature of the crime — sex and violence sold papers even back then — but also because of the context of the case."

Joseph pulled out a cigarette and gave the Digger a questioning glance. "What context was that?"

"The East End in those days was a tinderbox. In the midst of London's enormous wealth was the most abject poverty you could imagine. The kind that forces mothers to sell their children on the streets. And into this cauldron there were thousands of even poorer Jews coming every week from the ghettos of Poland and Russia — Jews who knew not a word of English, who wore strange clothes, who ate strange food. And who were often looked upon by the Christian community as Christ-killers one and all."

"Sounds like the makings of a pogrom," said Joseph.

The Digger nodded. "You put your finger on it, Radkin. The great fear among those in the know, who were following what was going on in Europe at the time, was exactly that — in what they considered to be the most civilized country in Europe there was the possibility of the kind of genocidal riots that were happening in the barbarous east. Something the Lipski case had focused attention on. Because here was a Jew who killed an Angel — and a pregnant one at that!"

"But she must have been Jewish, too . . ." said Joseph.

"Ah, but so was Christ. And don't think that many Cockneys didn't pick up on the symbolism. A typical insult of the day when you saw a Jew was to call him 'Lipski' and throw a rock."

"So Stead took up the gauntlet — is that what you're trying to say?"

"In a way. Stead was a complicated man. He was a radical thinker but also a keen businessman."

"You mean he knew what sold papers."

"Right. The Lipski case was news. But I think he also came to believe the man was innocent."

"How so?"

"First, because of his character. Lipski impressed most

people at his trial with his demeanor. He seemed to be a man of dignity. Second, because there was no real motivation; the prosecution could only come up with was a vague theory of lust. Third, the trial was a farce. Many of the witnesses, as well as Lipski himself, only spoke Yiddish. The best the court could provide was a translator who spoke German. And fourth, after the trial, stories began to circulate about witnesses who hadn't come forward and evidence suppressed by the police."

"Sounds like an interesting story," said Joseph. "Just the kind I'd take up myself. But I still don't understand the relationship to the Maybrick case or why Mike thought it so important."

"You know there wasn't any appellate court back then—not for criminal cases," said the Digger.

"Yeah, the only appeal was through the Home Office in the name of the Queen, I understand."

"After Lipski was sentenced and condemned to hang," the Digger went on, "the movement for reprieve—orchestrated in the main by the *Pall Mall Gazette* — grew louder. Stead, you see, was convinced the Lipski case could serve as a focus on the whole issue of criminal appeal."

"You mean the struggle for Lipski's reprieve also became a fight for a criminal appeal act?"

"That and other issues as well. The government had been tottering on the Irish question. Stead was looking for a scandal that could push them over the brink."

"So what happened?" asked Joseph.

"What happened is that in the final hour, the rug, so to speak, was pulled out. As Lipski's gallows were being built, word came that he confessed . . ."

"Confessed to the murder of Miriam Angel? Was the confession written out?"

"In English, of course. A language Lipski barely knew. To be fair, of course, Lipski had stated publicly that he would rather die than spend his life in prison. But the effect of the confession was to send the campaign for criminal appeal into a nose dive."

"I bet it didn't do much for Stead and the *Pall Mall Gazette*, either," Joseph said.

"Stead caved in immediately. Said he had made a grave mistake. And that's why he was relatively quiet on the Maybrick case. But there were others, like William Morris, who weren't as sure. He wrote a brilliant editorial for the *Commonweal* on the problem of accepting confessions of people on the brink of death . . ." The Digger suddenly stopped at the corner of a dreary-looking street. "Here we are," he said.

"Where?" asked Joseph, looking around at the tired brick buildings, pressed together like cold and lonely strangers searching for some warmth.

"Batty Street. Where the murder took place. Number Sixteen doesn't exist any more. Torn down in 1888, the very next year."

"Did you take Mike here?" asked Joseph.

"Yes." The Digger turned to him. He seemed to be studying his face. Then he said, "Do you believe in ghosts?"

"In a way," Joseph admitted, feeling a little shiver despite himself. "Not evil spirits, mind you — more like resonant memories . . ."

"Your friend Mike did."

Joseph looked at him curiously. "How so?"

"The two men who Lipski had accused — one was named Schmuss. By all accounts, he was a dour, solitary man. After the trial he took off for Birmingham. The other was a man named Rosenbloom. Both of them, like Lipski, were Polish immigrants. Some years later an English journalist reported that Rosenbloom had gone to America to start a new life. He had become enormously wealthy but, according to the journalist, was a tormented man. In 1920 he was said to have committed suicide . . ."

"That, in itself, means nothing," said Joseph.

"Right," the Digger said. "In fact, it's only a rumor. It may not even have been true. But it meant something to Rose."

"Why?" asked Joseph.

"Because like many people who went to America, Rosen-bloom anglicized his name by shortening it. So, it seems, did Mike's grandfather."

Joseph opened his eyes wide. "You mean Mike suspected that one of the men Lipski accused was actually his grandpa?"

The Digger nodded. "I got that feeling — yes."

"That's ridiculous!" said Joseph.

"Perhaps to you," said the Digger with a shrug. "But Rose became obsessed with the case. It was as if it became his personal responsibility to clear Lipski's name — and, by extension, that of Florence Maybrick."

"I don't understand," said Joseph, shaking his head. "What's this got to do with Maybrick?"

"Well, there were three key people who figured promi-nently in both the Lipski and the Maybrick case and one who almost did: Stead, of course, then the Home Secretary, the Judge, and the Hangman."

"I know Matthews was the Home Secretary," said Joseph. "And the judge in the Maybrick case was James Fitzjames Stephen. Who was Lipski's hangman?"

"A curious bloke named Berry. Something of an intel-lectual, he was. Did things like compute the maximum length of rope a man of a certain weight could have around his neck without jerking his head off by the drop. He even wrote a book about his life."

"This hangman," Joseph said, rubbing his chin, "was his first name James?"

"That's right. You know of him, then . . ."

"Yes," said Joseph. "It seems there's a lodge named after him."

"I wouldn't be surprised," said the Digger. "But the man Rose wanted to pursue was Stephen."

"He was the judge in both the trials?"

"Yes. The 'Mad Judge' some people say."

Joseph reached in his pocket and pulled out the photo of the executed animal he carried with him. "What do you make of this?" he asked.

The Digger took a glance and handed it back. "Rose showed it to me. He claimed someone sent it to him in the post. Where did you get it?"

"I found it in Mike's desk. You saw the inscription on the back — 'The Jews are the men that will not be blamed for nothing?'"

"Yes," the Digger said, "I saw it. But the word isn't 'Jews', it's 'Juwes'. It's a quote. Something that was supposedly left on the wall by Jack the Ripper."

"Good God!" said Joseph. "He's not involved in this too!"

"Well, this was his stomping ground," said the Digger. "It was only a year or so after Lipski was hanged. There were many who were convinced, back then, in that cauldron of depraved poverty, that the Ripper killings were done by the Jews as both part of the blood ritual and as revenge for Lipski's execution. The story goes that the police superintendent who saw the message chalked on the wall after one of the murders, had it erased to prevent a riot. But there are some who think it wasn't that at all . . ."

"What do they think, then?"

"That 'Juwes' doesn't refer to Jews, but to a Masonic rite which involves the three so-called Juwes — Jubeli, Jubelee, and Jubelum — and has to do with the ritual execution of those who betray the Masonic law: a ritual execution, by the way, very similar to the kind the Ripper performed on his victims. And would you like to know who one author chose as his prime suspect in the Ripper Case?"

Joseph sighed. "I suppose."

The Digger smiled like the Cheshire Cat. "Judge Stephen's son."

Chapter 14

The rains had started up again by the time he got back to his rooms and he wondered what proportion of their life people here spent cold and wet. There was a note on the little table just inside the entryway from Mrs White, saying she had gone to visit her sister for a few days and would he be kind enough to water the geraniums. He hoped, for her sake, Mrs White's sister lived someplace warm. Someplace like Tahiti or Madrid. But chances were she lived in County Cork. He shook himself off like a mangy dog and made his way upstairs.

No one had fixed the light in the hallway yet. No one was around to fix it, he supposed. Unless the neighborhood burglar had come back and decided to do a little repair work. But that wasn't the way of the world, he thought, as he knocked at his door.

Knocking at his own door didn't come easily to Joseph. He was more the type who fell through any old opening in the wall — whether he was invited to or not. But he thought it only right to give anyone waiting a fighting chance. After all, he told himself, they'd expect the same from him.

Of course, no one responded. They wouldn't be that dumb. He realized that. But ritual was ritual. He stuck his head inside and called out: "Hello? Anyone home?"

Again, no reply. Well, he tried. They had to say that for him. Always give a sucker an even break. That was his motto. But it was easy to be magnanimous when there was nobody else around, he thought, as he headed for the couch.

He dropped himself down on the cushions, lit up a cigarette and pondered the ceiling as he took a long and grateful puff. He listened to the rain pelting down onto the windows for a while and sighed. What was he doing here, cold and lonely and wet? What was any of this to him? Why didn't he just pack his toothbrush and take the first plane home? Why, for heaven's sake, didn't Mike? He was no fool. At least, Joseph didn't think he was.

But there was nothing more compelling to him than a half-completed story. It was easy to give up if you hadn't started yet. And it was easy to forget when you were done. But once he started, he was like a mule — an arrogant, pigheaded mule. A mule who wore blinders and couldn't see anything except what was straight ahead. And a nearsighted mule at that.

He picked up the phone at the side of the couch and dialed his number. An unfamiliar voice answered the phone.

"Hello? Radkin residence," it said.

"Hello. This is Radkin. Joseph type. Who's this?"

"Oh . . . Mr Radkin. Uh, this is Sue . . . the babysitter."

"Hello, Sue-the-babysitter. Does this mean my wife is out."

"She's out, Mr Radkin. Can I leave her a message?"

"Just tell her that I've been at the pool all day trying to improve my suntan."

"Gee, that's swell, Mr Radkin! Where are you, Acapulco?"

"Better than that, Sue. I'm at the North Pole."

"I didn't think it gets that warm there, Mr Radkin. What should I really tell your wife?"

"Tell her I love her. Tell her I miss her. Tell her I hope to be home soon."

After he hung up the phone, he lit another cigarette and pondered the ceiling again. He finished his smoke and closed his eyes. He pictured a field of golden buttercups. He was there with Polly and the kids. It was warm and sweet. And then he fell asleep.

The pounding at the door made him jolt upright. He glanced at his watch. It was ten after two. He shook himself. The pounding continued.

"Radkin! I know you're in there! Open up!"

He rubbed his eyes. "Who is it?"

"God damn it! Open up! Or I'll break the fucking door down!"

Rolling from the couch onto the floor, he righted himself and then grabbed the nearest heavy object, a table lamp, and jerking loose the cord, he went over to the door.

"I'm opening it now," he said. "Put away your gun."

He pulled open the door. There they stood. Wearing black slickers. Drenched in rain.

"What are you doing with that fucking lamp?" Chancellor said.

"Nothing," Joseph replied, putting it down.

Chancellor threw him some black rain gear. "Here! Put this on!" he commanded.

Joseph looked at Kate. She wasn't smiling. Then, again, she rarely was.

He put on the rain gear, a slicker and a pair of Wellingtons. "We going fishing?" he asked.

"You might say that, Sunshine," Chancellor replied.

Joseph followed them down the stairs, still a little bleary-eyed, and out into the rain.

Chancellor's Mini was parked next to the house. They piled in — Kate in the back, the two men in the front. The cold, wet engine took a while to start, but after playing with the choke, the engine turned over and Chancellor took off.

"I'd hate to use this as a getaway car," said Joseph.

"Careful what you say," said Chancellor. "You might have to."

Joseph turned to the back. "Care to tell me what's going on?"

Kate glared at him. Her lips were tight.

He turned to Chancellor. "Thanks for the bump on the head, by the way."

"Just do what I tell you and you won't get hurt!"

He turned back to Kate. "That's what my mother used to say."

"Your mother should get the martyr-of-the-century award," said Kate.

131

Joseph put his hands behind his head and stretched out — as far as the cramped space would allow. "It's really great going out on a picnic with friends," he said.

"Can't you take anything seriously?" Kate said in a tone of extreme annoyance.

"If I took things seriously, I would have hit you with the lamp." Joseph looked at Chancellor. "If we're going out for a midnight drink, I might remind you that this country closes tighter than a drum at twelve. The Queen wants all her kiddies to get to work on time."

Chancellor turned sharply at the top of Hampstead High Street and then left again, down a small road.

He brought the car up to the curb and cut the engine. He pulled the emergency brake and then blew on his fingers and put his hands together to rub out the cold. Pulling a bottle from his jacket pocket, Chancellor took a long drink before holding it out to Joseph. "Take a swig of this," he said.

Joseph put the bottle to his lips and swallowed. The brandy tasted raw. He made a face as he handed the bottle to Kate.

Kate took a drink and then handed the bottle back to Chancellor, who screwed on the top and put it back in his jacket pocket.

Rubbing the fog from the window and pressing his nose against the glass, Joseph looked out. He recognized the iron fence and leafy trees. He'd been there before. In fact, quite recently.

"I was afraid this was where you were heading," he said, shaking his head.

"Bloody bright, isn't he?" said Chancellor, looking back at Kate.

"Bright as the shine on his bum," said Kate.

Joseph wrinkled his brow in annoyance and said, simply, "Why?"

"Thought maybe you'd like to say your last farewell."

"In the States we tend to say our final goodbyes before someone's six feet underground," Joseph replied.

Chancellor opened up the door and got out. The rain was

still pouring down. He hunched up his shoulders and then looked back at the two inside. "Good weather," he said. "Makes the ground moist. Easy to dig . . ."

"What if someone happens to come by?" asked Joseph, getting out, too, and pulling the rain hood over his top. "What are you going to tell them? That you lent your keys to someone who was buried yesterday and you're just trying to get them back?"

"We'll be at the far end of the graveyard — well out of sight. No one's going to see. Besides, who's going to be out walking at three in the morning in all this rain?"

"Us," said Joseph.

Kate, meanwhile, was squeezing herself out from the back seat. Catching her foot on the side of the door, she tripped, tumbling toward the pavement. Joseph caught her before she hit the ground. He lifted her up, and as he did, he saw the wetness in her eyes — which wasn't rain.

Chancellor, meanwhile, was unloading the back of the car. He took out a bag of tools from the boot and then reached inside and grabbed two garden spades which lay crossways on the back-seat floor.

Loaded down with his equipment, he turned and gave Joseph a hard look. "Coming?" he asked.

Joseph shook his head. "I'm allergic to resurrections," he said, taking out a cigarette and trying to light it in the pouring rain. "Once every two thousand years is enough."

He could see the muscles in Chancellor's face tighten and, as if forcing himself back into control, quickly relax again. "Suit yourself," he said, in a tone of disgust. "Just give a whistle if you see someone come along."

Theft was one thing, Joseph thought, as he watched the two of them walk off into the soggy burial ground; robbing graves was quite another. He felt squeamish enough when, helping Polly plant her flowers, he cut into a worm by accident. The idea of digging up a coffin in the dead of night and opening it, whatever Chancellor's insane reason could be, was not something he had any strong desire to support. Even by a whistle.

133

He watched them through the iron gate, their silhouettes illuminated faintly by the pale moon shining through the rain. He could see Chancellor trudging along, and Kate, buffeted by the wind, walking at his side, like the tattered sail of a pirate ship in a poorly produced school play.

Leaning his weight against the front of the Mini, he wondered how he could have ended up out here in the pouring rain. He wondered what Polly would say if he had guts enough to tell her. And then he thought about Mike, laid to rest by his neurotic mother, now probably well on the way to disinterment for reasons only Kate and Chancellor knew. He wondered what the authorities would say. Perhaps just being there was grounds for deportation.

He finished his soggy cigarette and crushed it under his heel. He tried to light another, but it kept going out. He looked up at the sky and let the rain fall on his face for a while. Then he looked down the road. He could barely see the streetlights of Hampstead High Street, even though it was only a stone's throw away. Listening closely, he thought he could hear the sound of feet. His heart skipped a beat. What if it was a cop? Shouldn't he have an explanation ready? What was he doing here, parked by the graveyard in the middle of a rainy night? Taking a midnight bath? Was that his car? Did he have registration papers? Keys? Of course not. It wasn't his. He was just standing here, that's all. What if they told him to move on? So what? Why was he staying there anyway?

"Radkin!"

He nearly shit at the sound of the voice from behind. It was Chancellor. His face was dripping with rainwater mixed with sweat. His trousers were caked with mud.

"Jesus!" he said. "You scared me half to death!"

"You frighten easily, Sunshine! Did you wet your pants?"

"Yeah, I usually do when I'm standing in the rain. I'm not a fuckin' duck!"

Chancellor mopped his forehead with the back of his arm. "Come on," he said, "I need your help. Kate is too bloody small to lift the coffin."

"I could have told you that. Why didn't you just hire someone from a temporary agency? Graverobbers Associates —I hear they're good."

"This isn't fun for me either, Sunshine," he said, staring at him intently.

"So why don't we go home?" asked Joseph, pointing toward the car.

The elder man ground his teeth. "Lavinia can't go home. Neither can I."

"But how the hell is digging up Mike's body going to help her?"

"Do I have to spell it out to you?"

"Yes."

He could see the steam from Chancellor's breath as he spoke. "I think Rose was killed by the same person who killed Fry."

"OK," said Joseph, "so let's say he was. What does that prove?"

"It proves that Lavinia didn't kill Fry because she was already in prison when Rose was bumped off."

"So you're digging up Mike's body on a hunch?" Joseph looked at him in amazement.

Chandler stared back with the kind of determination usually reserved for bulls in Spanish colosseums. "It's a good hunch, Radkin." Then, in a softer voice, he said, "Don't make me beg . . ."

Looking at the big man's eyes, Joseph felt his obstinacy give way. "OK," he said with a sigh, "but this better fuckin' be worth it or I'm charging you twice my going rate!"

He followed Chancellor through the iron gate and back to the spot where Mike had been buried. Kate was standing near a mound of mud, leaning against her shovel. Her face was streaked with dirt. She appeared to him like a tigress who had been pursued all night by hunters, only to be trapped, exhausted, in a cemetery, with nowhere left to run.

As they approached, her eyes were blazing. "I could have done it!" she hissed, foamy water trickling from her mouth.

135

"You've got the muscle," Chancellor said, "but not enough meat on your bones."

Joseph noticed that they had set up a neat little tackle-and-pulley device, using one of the nearby monuments to support the weight. The heavy rope led from there, down into the hole and was tied to another pulley-and-hook device which, in turn, was connected to leather straps fitted around the coffin.

Chancellor wasted no time, using the rope to slide into the grave — quite lithely, Joseph thought, for a man of his age.

"I could have done it myself," Chancellor said hoarsely, "if it wasn't for the rain. The damn thing's stuck in the mud!"

As Joseph and Kate tugged at the rope, Chancellor tried to lift from below. But, as the storm had yet to subside, he kept sinking in the mud, till only his head and torso showed.

"Pull!" His voice had a sandpaper rasp. "Pull that bloody rope!"

Kate's hands were already dripping with blood, and tears streamed from her eyes — more from frustration than from pain, Joseph thought. He, too, was putting all his weight into the task, but the mud was sucking like a toilet plunger, drawing the coffin back into the grave.

Chancellor's shoulders were now under the mud as well. He was in it up to his chin. Sensing the danger, Kate lifted herself up the rope and putting her feet against the monument as leverage, gave a mighty tug. It caused such a lurch that Joseph lost control and fell with his hand still tied around the rope. But the combination of events was enough to break the coffin from the grip of the swollen earth.

"Don't let it fall back, whatever you do!" shouted Chancellor, grabbing the strap and pulling himself free. "It should be better now."

Sure enough, once the coffin was released from the mud, it came up quite easily. When it was level to the ground, they tied it down, throwing the excess rope to Chancellor so he could climb back up.

Having made it safely out of the grave, Chancellor stumbled over to the monument. He sounded as if he was gasping for air.

"Are you all right, Ron?" Kate asked, coming over to him and kneeling down by his side.

"Nothing to worry about," he said, his breathing under control once more. "Slight case of emphysema." Pointing to his canvas bag, he said. "Bring that over here."

Kate lugged it over and Chancellor, still seated, opened it up, withdrawing some tools. Then, standing again, he directed them to swing the coffin till it was over firm ground. The tackle was undone and the belts around the coffin untied.

Chancellor now went back to his canvas bag and took out an all-weather lantern. He handed it to Joseph and looked at him hard. "Keep it trained on the top. Understand? Whatever happens, don't let it budge! If you lift it one inch, the caretaker will see and we'll be bloody well done!"

Joseph nodded. It was too far along for him to argue. All he could do was watch this gruesome scene with morbid fascination.

As he kept the light fixed on the coffin top, albeit shakily, Chancellor began to undo the screws. Kate stood by, like a nurse in an operating theatre, taking the brass fasteners as he handed them to her.

He still wasn't breathing properly, Joseph thought. His breath came in short gasps. But this wasn't the time or place to do a medical report. Ill or not, Chancellor moved easily and seemed to get more energy as each succeeding screw came out.

Joseph felt his head grow light as the last of the fasteners were twisted loose and handed to Kate. He felt himself in a warm sweat while, at the same time, shivering with cold.

"Hold that damn light straight, I told you!" Chancellor said in a whispered shout.

Joseph held the torch in both hands as Chancellor took a hammer and chisel and began to tap around the lid.

Kate was by Joseph's side now, watching, as he did, with a strange, hypnotic stare. There was something horribly fascinating about this macabre event. He felt it in his stomach as well as in the prickling of his skin. All he could see was the coffin lid. All he could hear was the rhythmic tapping as Chancellor gently moved the chisel out and then in.

He was barely aware that Kate had slid her hand in his. He could barely feel the heat of her skin.

And then suddenly it happened. There was an awesome sound. Like the earth was opening up and they were all falling in. The coffin lid flew off. And like a horrific Jack-in-the-box, the body lurched up toward them. Joseph froze in terror. His heart had stopped beating, but he couldn't avert his gaze. Yet all he could see was that face, that terrible, hideous face, now only inches from his own, wearing the most revolting, contorted grin.

The odor that came with this sickening event was the worst stench he had ever smelled. He turned and retched. And then he retched again.

He felt a claw of iron turn him round. The claw of iron forced him to gaze down once more on that terrifying mask of death.

"Look, you bloody bastard! Look!" the voice hissed. "The smile! You see the smile? Fix it in your bloody mind! 'Risus sardonicus' it's called. The devil's laugh! It's the mark of strychnine poisoning! You understand?"

He pulled himself from Chancellor's grasp and turned around. He didn't see her at first.

"Kate!" he called out.

And then he saw. She had fainted dead away and was lying silent on the ground.

Chapter 15

They were back in the Mini again, beating a hasty retreat toward Gospel Oak after a quick reburial ceremony.

"It'll take some time to get that face out of my mind," said Joseph. He turned to Chancellor. "'Risus sardonicus' you say? In my dictionary, sardonic means 'to mock'. Maybe they should rename it 'Risus frighten-your-ass-off'. No wonder Kate passed out."

"I didn't faint," said Kate, somewhat defensively. "I was hit by the coffin lid."

"That's what I meant," Joseph replied. Looking back at Chancellor, he asked, "What the hell causes someone to look like that anyway?"

"It's the effect of strychnine on the central nervous system," Chancellor replied. "It causes violent muscular spasms which end in the victim strangulating himself to death. After death, the muscles of the corpse become grossly contracted causing the strange facial expression. It also means the back is severely arched, making the body into a coiled spring. They probably had to sit on that damn coffin lid to nail him in."

"Not the most pleasant way to die, I guess," Joseph said.

"What way is?" Chancellor muttered between his teeth.

Joseph glanced over at the tough man driving. "What about that autopsy report you showed me?"

"What about it?"

"Seems to me the rigor mortis was a little more than 'peculiar'."

"Maybe someone's trying to cover something up."

"Who?" asked Joseph, watching the muscles in Chancellor's face tighten.

"You tell me, Sunshine!"

He turned into Rona Road and pulled over to the side.

Kate leaned forward. "You want to come in? I'll fix you something hot to drink."

Chancellor shook his head. "Not now." His voice sounded weary. "I need some sleep. I'll phone you later today."

They got out of the car. Chancellor revved the tiny engine of the Mini and sped off.

The rain had subsided. The sky was growing light.

"Good-night," said Joseph, waving his hand at Kate. "Or good-morning, should I say. And don't think I didn't have a good time . . ." He started walking across the street. "I'm sure glad Mrs White is out of town," he said, looking down at his muddy tracks.

"Radkin!" she called out.

He turned around. Tears were streaming from her eyes. He walked back to where she was.

She shook her head. "I can't stay there alone," she said.

"Where's Sean?" he asked.

She motioned toward the upstairs. "They took him to the country for a few days." Suddenly, she buried her head in his shoulder and began to sob.

He stroked her hair. "That's all right, Kate," he said. "Let it out. You can be tough and cry at the same time."

"No I can't."

"Yes, you can. Anyway, no one can see you."

"Except you," she sobbed.

"Just pretend I'm not here."

She looked up at him. Her face was streaked with mud and tears. "Do you always have to play the fool?" she asked.

"Not always," he replied. A moment later, in a softer tone, he said, "You loved him, didn't you?"

"I don't know." She shook her head.

"It doesn't matter," said Joseph. "Everything is forgotten if you leave it long enough."

She shook her head again. "No. I'll never forget that face.

140

Not as long as I live." She looked up at him. "Don't leave me alone. Not tonight."

He put his arm around her shoulder. "All right, Kate. I'll stay with you, if that's what you want. You can come over to my place or I'll go to yours. Whatever you want."

"My place," she said. "Please . . ."

"OK," he replied.

They walked over to her house and she opened the door.

"Take your clothes off," she said.

He looked at her, amazed at her abruptness.

"The mud," she said. "Don't worry. I've seen naked men before. I bathe Sean every day."

They took their clothes off in the entryway.

"What am I going to put on?" he asked her. "My clean stuff is back there," he said, pointing across the street.

"I have some things you can wear," she said. She looked at him and he saw a slight smile. "You're caked in mud. The bathroom's upstairs," she said. "Why don't you wash yourself off?"

He went upstairs and washed himself with the hand-held shower spray, shampooing his hair and letting the crusted earth from Mike's burial ground run down the drain.

After a soothing warm rinse, which felt like heaven after a quick trip to hell, he toweled himself dry and stuck his head out the door. Kate had left a neat pile of clothes on the other side: shirt, trousers, underwear, socks and pajamas. He put on the pajamas. They were a perfect fit.

"Tell me when you're done," he heard her call out. "There's some hot coffee waiting for you downstairs. Fresh ground."

"I'm done," he said, already half-way to the living-room.

She looked at him and smiled. "You look very nice," she said. "Here're some biscuits and cheese. There's more stuff in the fridge. Take whatever you want. I'm going upstairs to have a bath."

He had his coffee and ate the cheese and crackers. Perhaps it was the jolt from the caffeine, but suddenly he began to feel shaky again. Something felt very odd. There was a strange taste in his mouth.

He stood up and then he sat back down on the couch. His head was spinning. He looked up. He saw her standing there. She was dressed in a flowing nightgown. She looked like an angel come to take him to a land far beyond the seas.

"Coming to bed?" she asked.

He rubbed his head. "I feel a little dizzy, Kate."

She came up beside him and put her soft hand on his temple. "You feel warm," she said. "You're tired. You need some sleep."

He looked up into her eyes.

"Is that what you told Mike?" he asked.

"Sometimes . . ." she replied.

"Did you fix him coffee, too?"

"Sometimes . . ."

She bent down and he felt her moist lips on his forehead. "Come," she said, "it's time to rest."

His head was spinning. What a lovely way to die, he thought as he tried to stand. And then everything went blank.

The sun was beaming through the window when he awoke and tossed the covers off. He rubbed his eyes and looked around. He was in Kate's living-room. Still on the couch.

There was a pot of coffee and a note waiting for him on the table. He poured himself some coffee and glanced at the note. "You were exhausted, I guess. You collapsed on the couch. I had some things to do. See you later? Love, Kate."

There was a throbbing in his head as he stood up. An echo, he supposed, from yesterday. He looked at his watch. It was something past two in the afternoon.

He reached for the clothes Kate had left for him, which she had placed on a chair by the couch. He put them on and wondered, again, at the near-perfect fit. Then, grabbing his jacket, he went out the door.

There was something Joseph didn't like. Something he hated, in fact. He hated being used. And something told him that there was a scene being played out behind his back; a scene in which he was very much involved.

It was, he thought, like a jigsaw puzzle that had been thrown into the air with little bits and pieces landing everywhere. To collect them all was a task in itself. To put it together was insane.

He walked to South End Green and then up Hampstead hill.

He had checked the address in his notebook. Sure enough, she lived in the fanciest house on the block. It was one of those mansions that try to coexist with the lesser stuff, but don't quite succeed in blending in. First of all, it took up two plots of land instead of one. And second, it was set back from the road, much further than the other millionaire showplaces which tried like hell to pretend they were still part of the old Hampstead Bohemia by being more accessible to the postman, and not having him hike so far to put their monthly dividend checks into the letter box.

There was a circular drive which led to the entrance of the house. Joseph walked quickly down the path and up the grand staircase to the front door, where he proceeded to press his weight against the buzzer.

He was met by the butler — a balding guy who, as far as he could tell, had taken elocution lessons from P. G. Wodehouse.

"May I say who's calling, sir?" he asked.

"You may," said Joseph.

The butler looked at him a moment without changing the expression on his face.

"Who's calling, sir?"

"A friend of her son's."

"And do you have a name?"

"I do."

"Then who's calling, sir?"

"It's Joseph Radkin calling — but not for Philip Morris."

143

The butler didn't crack a smile.

"You're probably too young to remember that," said Joseph.

"I'll see if she's in, sir," said the butler.

Joseph quickly pushed himself through the opening before the butler could shut the door. He smiled. "I'm sure she wouldn't mind if I waited inside."

The butler raised his eyebrows but didn't throw him out. "Please wait there, sir, while I find out if Madame is seeing visitors this afternoon."

"She'll see me," Joseph advised as he watched the butler disappear into another room.

While the butler was away chasing up Madame, Joseph took a little look around. The place was certainly fancy enough for your standard Royal tea, he thought. But, never having been to one, he couldn't say for sure. He was standing in a rather ornate hall with oak walls and heavy pictures of tired old bats who all looked like they had hernias. A circular stairway led up to the sky — at least to a second floor, anyhow. There was the requisite crystal chandelier hanging from the ceiling, with enough baubles tinkling from it that it was sure to make a hell of a crash if it ever did fall down.

"La-de-da!" he heard himself say. He turned to look some more. Then something on a little table by the wall caught his eye. Some mail was piled there and a letter atop the pile had been propped up. On the upper left-hand corner was a crest — a crest he had seen before. He walked over and picked the letter up.

"Mr Radkin . . ."

As he heard the butler call his name, he slipped the letter into his pocket.

". . . I'm afraid Mrs Hughes isn't seeing anyone this afternoon."

He turned to face him. "I've got something very important to tell her . . ."

The butler shook his head.

"I'm afraid not."

"It's about her son."

"She isn't seeing anyone today, Mr Radkin. Mrs Hughes is ill. She's confined to bed. Next time, perhaps you should call for an appointment." He put a white gloved hand on Joseph's shoulder.

Joseph shoved it off. "Bullshit!" he said angrily. Facing the circular stairs, he shouted, "Mrs Hughes? I know you're up there, Mrs Hughes! Listen to me! Mike was killed! He wasn't run over by a truck . . ."

The butler grabbed him more forcefully this time. "That'll be all, buster!" he said, sounding more like a bouncer in a café.

Joseph shoved him aside again. "Well, maybe he was run over by a truck, Mrs Hughes. Maybe he was. But he was poisoned, too! And I think you know why!" he shouted at the top of his lungs.

The butler wasn't playing any games now. He wrenched Joseph's arm behind his back. "You'll get out of here fast, if you know what's good for you!" he said, dropping the fancy pear-shaped tones and moving Joseph over to the door.

"Hey," said Joseph. "You're American!"

"What's it to you?" growled the butler, opening the door and pushing him out.

"Nothing," said Joseph, as the door slammed in his face. "I was just going to applaud your performance. But, fuck it! If you're going to be that way, I'm not even going to write a review!"

He walked back to Gospel Oak with his hands in his pockets. He sometimes found it a good way to think. Nothing added up. Not that it ever came easy to him. But he could usually put two and two together without coming up with twelve.

He tried knocking at Kate's door when he got to Rona Road. She wasn't in. She wasn't answering, anyway. Maybe she was in bed with Mrs Hughes. Who knows? he thought. Stranger things had happened.

He walked across the street to his rooms. He looked up and

saw the curtain from his window flutter in the wind. He couldn't remember opening the window, but maybe he did. Maybe he did a lot of things unconsciously.

The hallway light still wasn't fixed as he made his way upstairs. But he didn't knock at his own door this time. He was tired of knocking. He had done enough knocking at doors. It was time to settle things now.

He reached into his jacket pocket and pulled out the letter that he had copped at the Hughes mansion. The crest he had recognized was from Foxton Manor. The envelope had already been opened and had probably been left propped up there as a reminder.

Inside was a notice. It read: "The Annual Hunt has been rescheduled so as not to be inconvenienced by the anarchists. The meeting place has been changed to the Hare and the Hound. Please arrive five a.m. promptly. For security reasons, please wear a white carnation. And remember, no cameras of any kind are permitted." The note was signed: "For the Hunt Committee, R. Palmerston."

Joseph put the note back inside the envelope and stuck it in his pocket. Then he went to the telephone and dialed. He listened as it rang several times before a voice came on the line:

"McIssacs here."

"Hi, it's Radkin. Find anything out?"

"James Berry was a hangman . . ."

"I know that. Anything else?"

"Foxton Manor. It's near Newmarket — not too far from the race-track. And you know who it belongs to?"

"Palmerston. Anything else?"

"Strykill — it's a potent pesticide used for larger mammalian predators — weasels, foxes, raccoons . . ."

"Main ingredient, strychnine?"

"Yes."

"You need a license?"

"Can only be sold to farmers, I believe."

"Find out who manufactures it?"

"Zenith Chemicals."

146

"Mean anything to you?"

"I looked it up. Seems it's a subsidiary of Hughes Industries."

"OK!" said Joseph, jotting something down.

"Are you going to tell me what this is all about?"

"Soon, I hope," said Joseph. "One more thing, by the way . . ."

He heard McIssacs sigh. "You want to know about the virgin birth . . ."

"Not that simple," he said. "I'd like you to find out what you can about a man named Singh — it's spelled S-i-n-g-h. He's a doctor."

"What kind of a doctor?"

"How the hell should I know?"

"You don't ask much, do you?"

"I'll treat you to a bottle of grappa when you're done."

"I'd appreciate that," said McIssacs. "I'll use it to get the spots out of my clothes — from all your bloodletting."

"You want to be an investigative journalist, don't you?"

"How did you know that?"

"Lucky guess. Anyway what's a little bloodletting between friends?" asked Joseph. And then he hung up the phone.

He hadn't set the receiver down on it's cradle for more than an instant when the telephone rang.

"Mortuary services," he answered. "Graves dug up, bodies disinterred — no charge for estimates."

"How did you know it was me?" she said.

"I didn't," he replied. "Where are you calling from?"

"Home," said Kate.

"I knocked at your door just five minutes ago."

"I was in the bath . . ."

"Again? You took one last night!"

"I like to keep clean. Don't you?"

"Not that clean," he said. "By the way, what did you put in my coffee?"

"Why? Didn't you like it? It was fresh."

"I'm not disputing the freshness, Kate . . ."

"Then what do you mean?"

"Never mind," he said. "I'd like to talk to you about something."

"What?"

"Not over the phone," he said. "Mind if I come around?"

"Why not? You already slept in my bed."

"You mean the couch. I didn't sleepwalk last night, did I?"

"No, but you snore like a lumberjack saws trees."

"Sorry. I'll wear a muzzle next time. See you in a jiff . . ."

He knocked at her door. Her hair was wrapped in a towel when she opened up. "Hello," she said. "Come in."

There was no trace of their midnight party except for a blue plastic bag she pointed out. "Your clothes. I hope they're not ruined," she said.

"Just throw them in the garbage," he said. "I don't think I could wear them again."

"That's what I did with mine," she admitted, sitting down in the chair opposite the couch. "What did you want to talk about?"

He took out his cigarettes and lit one up. "You want a smoke?" he said.

She shook her head.

He took a long, determined puff and let it trail out of his mouth, all the while looking directly at her.

"Well?" she said, blinking her eyes. "Did you want to talk or look?"

"Both," he said. "Talk is cheap."

"You should know," said Kate.

"Let's get down to it, shall we?" he said.

"I thought we were."

"You haven't been what I call 'straight'."

"What do you call 'straight'?" she asked. "Or shouldn't I be bold?"

"By 'straight' I mean truthful, frank, undevious, unfraudulent."

148

"Then, by implication, I take it you're saying I've been a lying, devious fraud."

"Yes."

She took the towel off her head and rubbed her hair. "So what if I have?"

"Nothing," he replied. "I just thought we should put our cards on the table."

She put down her towel and fluffed up her hair with her hand. "Listen, Radkin," she said. "I've grown to like you. I didn't before . . ."

"Then why not be straight with me?" he said.

"OK," she sighed. "It's true we've been using you . . ."

"By 'we', you mean you and Chancellor?"

"Yes. We needed you to believe . . ."

"Believe what?"

"That Lavinia was innocent and that Mike knew who did it. We knew you'd follow his trail."

"Which is why you planted that stuff in Mike's room."

"Yes. But I didn't hit you that night."

"It was Chancellor, wasn't it?"

"He couldn't wait for you to find it on your own. He thought you'd need a little help."

"And you were watching from your window, right?"

"Yes."

"You phoned him when you saw me coming up."

"Yes. I thought he'd have time to get away."

"Down the drainpipe. He probably was out of breath. He's got a heart condition, you know."

"I didn't think he'd hit you," she said.

"Don't worry about it. I've got a hard head."

"You're telling me!"

"Where did the stuff come from, Kate? The microfilm, I mean."

"Ron found it in the desk of Lavinia's lout, pasted underneath a drawer. He's convinced Fry was blackmailing Palmerston."

"Over what?"

149

"We're not sure." She was fidgeting with her hair again.

"Do you know what the James Berry Memorial Lodge is all about?"

She shook her head. "No."

"And how about the purchase order for Strykill?"

"We're not sure about that, either. But it does show Palmerston had access to strychnine."

"Was Mike in on this too?"

She looked down at the floor for a moment and then back up at him. "I don't know. Ron came to me after Mike's death. He said he needed my help . . ."

"Did Chancellor take Mike's stuff?"

"Perhaps."

"Mike wasn't killed for nothing, Kate."

She wiped a tear from her eye. "I realize that."

He stubbed his cigarette out and said, "And you might be in danger, as well."

Chapter 16

Feed a monkey half a banana and he'll be satisfied. That's the difference between simians and the human race. Simians are smart. They'll take the half and move on. Humans want the whole thing — even if it's being used as bait.

Back in his room, Joseph took Mike's diary out and turned to the appropriate page. It was marked "Cambridge — R. R. S., Trinity". West said Mike had gone to Cambridge to meet a man named Snibley. Joseph picked up the receiver and phoned.

The train ride from Liverpool Street Station up to Cambridge was quicker than going around London on the Circle Line. The countryside that sped by was flat and green and all looked pretty much the same. The taxi ride from Cambridge Station took another fifteen minutes. Within an hour and a half of leaving London he was standing by the college gates.

It was like being transported to another world. It was quiet here and serene. No dirt, no litter and the people were scrubbed clean. Looking up at the college walls, built like fortress ramparts, and the cathedral-like buildings, rich with the symbols of power and privilege now reserved for banks, he felt a little ill-at-ease. Fortunately, several drunken students came by and parked their bikes. One went behind a tree and took a pee while the other puked his guts out in the middle of the road. So Joseph felt it probably was all right.

The college porter conducted him past the central quad and through an archway that led to the faculty residences and pointed the way to Snibley's door.

Snibley was a tall, angular man with bleary eyes and thick

stubble on his chin. He stooped in the doorway as he let Joseph in.

"Nice place," said Joseph, taking a quick glance around at all the ancient woody stuff he figured would cost a bundle in New York.

"I suppose so," said Snibley, a stub of a cigarette hanging out of his mouth. He ushered Joseph back into his study. "Hardy used to live here — the mathematician, that is. I keep finding bits and pieces of paper stuffed in the cracks . . ."

"His writings or what?"

"Old formulas . . . things like that."

"Oh."

Snibley took a bottle of whisky and two dirty glasses from the shelf. "Care for a drink? 'Fraid all I have is this bottle of Scotch. Had a blasted party here for new students the other night and now all my liquor's gone."

"I just saw two of them outside," said Joseph. "They're still drunk."

"Kids can't drink anymore," Snibley moaned. "Not like the old days, at least."

"No," said Joseph, holding up the glass and admiring the color, "but that just leaves more for us."

Snibley sat down in a chair and motioned for Joseph to do the same. "What is it you wanted to see me about?"

"A colleague of mine had a meeting with you a few weeks back. Rose was his name. His first name was Mike."

"Past tense?" asked Snibley, uncrossing his gangly legs and leaning slightly forward.

Joseph nodded. "Yeah."

Snibley took off his wire-rimmed spectacles and rubbed his bleary eyes. "He came to see me about Stephen — James Fitzjames. You know — the judge."

"Did he want to know anything in particular?"

"Said he was doing an article on several cases Stephen had tried and wanted background information on him."

"Why did he come to you?"

"Stephen's papers are here at the library. I'm supposed to be an authority of sorts — though heaven knows . . ."

"Could you give me a brief run down?" Joseph asked.

Snibley reached for a pack of Camels on his desk and lit up a smoke. It seemed to put his eyes back into focus. "What do you know about the man?"

"Not much," Joseph admitted.

"Came from an interesting family," said Snibley, crossing his legs again and spitting out a piece of tobacco that had been stuck against his tongue, "fascinating tale — like a Victorian dynasty. One uncle involved in the slave trade, another in cotton mills. Leslie, the brother, was the father of Virginia Woolf, you know."

"I didn't," said Joseph, taking notes.

"Streak of insanity in the family — down to modern day. Chap they caught a few years ago who cut up young men and hid the remains in drainpipes. He was related to the Stephens, as well."

"How about the judge — James Fitzjames?"

"Quite a reasonable fellow until he got old and dotty. But they kept him on the bench too long. Made a right mess of the Maybrick case. Treated it more like a biblical allegory than a trial . . ."

"I know."

"But the real loony was his son. Virginia Woolf mentions him in her letters. He had violent and uncontrollable fits of temper. Some say it was syphilis — which could explain Fitzjames' unlove of fallen women."

Joseph took the photo of the hanging goat from his pocket. "Did Mike show you this?" he asked.

"Yes . . . and the writing on the back."

"Do you know the theory that connects it to the Freemasons?"

"The Masons are ripe to be set up for anything, aren't they?" said Snibley. "Organizations that are shrouded in secrecy are open to any charge — even the most outlandish."

"You don't believe it, then?" asked Joseph.

153

Snibley shrugged and took another drink. "No reason why I should. Of course, there are always aberrations in any group. For example that psuedo-Masonic lodge in Italy — Propaganda Due. They had all manner of Government bigwigs in it — the Minister of Justice, judges, police chiefs. Gelli — the chap on top — collected a suitcase full of secrets and used it to blackmail all of them."

"He wanted to use it as a base for a coup, I understand."

"Most likely. But the real organization isn't like that," said Snibley.

"Maybe not," said Joseph. "However things like Propaganda Due show its potential." He took out the photo again and looked at Snibley. "Why do you think someone would write that on the back?"

"Perhaps they wanted your friend to believe there was a link between Jack the Ripper and the Masons. And, by extension, the same group and your Jack the Animal Killer . . ." Snibley suddenly stopped and rubbed his chin.

"Remember something?" Joseph asked.

"It just struck me — in medieval Europe they used to try animals for crimes, did you know that? Of course, that was before the Church decided animals had no soul."

"There's a cat who once ate my favorite canary," said Joseph. "It certainly had no soul! I wouldn't have minded seeing it sent up for birdslaughter."

"They held real trials back then — with lawyers and judges. Everything was the same, except, of course, the defendant, who might have been a pig or a goat."

Joseph thought a moment. Then he said, "Ever hear of the James Berry Memorial Lodge?"

Snibley shook his head.

"Newmarket is close to here, isn't it?"

"Just down Newmarket Road," Snibley replied. "Not more than a quarter-hour drive."

"How about the Palmerston mansion — Foxton Manor, I think it's called?"

"Not far from Newmarket. They have stables there."

"Do you know anything about the elder Palmerston — the judge?"

"They put him out to pasture some years ago. They do that here, you know. Judges get a bit dotty and then they let them graze a while before they bury them."

Joseph got up from his chair. "Thanks for taking the time to talk to me."

"Anything to avoid the eyestrain of reading student scratchings," said Snibley. "Hope I've been of help."

"By the way," asked Joseph, "any idea where Mike went after he visited you?"

"He said he had to meet some chap. Asked me if I knew anything about him."

"You remember his name?"

Snibley rubbed his head. "Indian chap, I believe. But I can't recall his name. I think he was a research scientist though."

"Up here in Cambridge?"

"No. I believe he was meeting him down in London," said Snibley, walking Joseph to the door.

"His name wasn't Singh, with an 'h' on the end, was it?"

"With an 'h' on the end? Yes, I think it was."

Joseph stood by the door and scratched his head.

"There's something else you have on your mind?" Snibley asked.

"There is . . ." said Joseph.

"You might as well let me in on it."

"Your name — what does the R. R. stand for?"

Snibley looked at him blankly and then replied, "My parents never told me and, to tell the truth, I never asked . . ."

Liverpool Street was only a few minutes' walk from Whitechapel Road, the heart of the East End. The card Mike's mother had given him said that Singh's address was on a small street between there and Commercial Road — just a stone's throw from where Lipski had lived.

155

Joseph found it without much difficulty. It was a three-story building of small apartments above a wholesale clothing shop. The outer door opened onto some stairs which led up from a common entryway. As he came in, two young Asian children ran past him, giggling, and then skirted out the door.

Inside, a pungent odor of spices and incense filled the hall and tingled his nostrils — in contrast to the sanitizing fluids that permeated the atmosphere in Mrs White's house and only made him sneeze.

Singh's apartment was on the second floor. To get to it, Joseph had to squeeze past a little boy with raven-black hair who was bouncing a rubber ball on the steps. Joseph found the door and knocked. He waited for a moment and then knocked again.

"No one's there," said the little boy, who had followed him up and was now staring at him with wide, curious eyes.

Joseph knelt down and smiled at the little fellow. "I can see that. What time does he get home, do you know?"

The little boy shrugged.

"Is your mama around?"

There was another shrug.

"Where do you live?" asked Joseph.

The boy turned and pointed to a door on the other side of the hall which, at that moment, opened up. A young woman with strikingly long hair, dressed in a sari, came out. She looked at Joseph suspiciously and then said something to the boy in a language Joseph couldn't understand. The boy ran quickly into her arms. She was about to usher him into the apartment when Joseph spoke up.

"Excuse me," he said. "Does Dr Singh live here?"

"Dr Singh?" asked the woman, repeating the name with a slightly different intonation.

Joseph took the card out of his pocket and displayed it to her. "I'm a colleague of his, you see. I was supposed to meet him. He gave me his card . . ."

"You're a friend?"

156

"A colleague," Joseph said. "We worked together. Dr Singh is a very brilliant man."

"Oh yes," the woman agreed. "A very brilliant man. He studied chemistry for many years."

"I know," said Joseph. "I've long been an admirer of his work. Has he ever told you about it? Fascinating, really."

"What kind of work is it?" she asked.

"Didn't he tell you?" said Joseph innocently.

"He was a quiet man," said the woman. "But very, very kind."

"I know he's had some unfortunate trouble," said Joseph. "I wanted to see if there was anything I could do to help him out."

"Yes," she said, "he's had much trouble. He was very much afraid . . ."

Joseph pointed to the door. "I've tried knocking. He doesn't seem to be in. Do you know what time he'll be back?"

"Dr Singh has gone away," she said.

"Yes, I know," said Joseph. "But when will he be back."

She shook her head. "No. He will not be back. Dr Singh has gone away for good."

"Do you know where I can reach him?" Joseph asked.

"If you wish to reach him," she said, "you will have to go to India." And saying that, she backed inside her apartment and latched the door.

He had picked up a wilted lettuce, a soggy tomato and some stale cheese at the Pakistani grocery before going up to his rooms. Now he sat in the dark and ate his three-course meal in silence.

The phone rang. He went to pick it up.

"Joseph!" she said. "I've been trying to reach you for days!"

"Oh, hi, Polly," he said. "I haven't been here much . . ."

"Sue told me you phoned. Something wrong?"

"Much is wrong. Little's right. This story's more complicated than I suspected."

"It always is, isn't it? Have you organized yourself? Did you make a chart and hang it on the wall?"

He looked over at the bare wall. "The landlady doesn't allow it," he said. "Seriously, though, Polly, I think I am onto something big."

"I bet that's what Mike said, too, before he was bumped off," she replied.

"I'm not going to get bumped off, Polly!" he said. "I told you not to worry."

"Thanks," she said. "Actually, the reason for the call was to tell you that I'm coming over."

"No you're not."

"Yes, I am. I have it all arranged with your mother. She's volunteered to watch the kids."

"So what are you going to do? Be my minder?"

"Maybe you need one."

"I can take care of myself."

"You mean you're really telling me not to come?"

"Yes."

There was silence at the other end of the line. Then she said, "Maybe I could help. Remember the Big Story? I helped you with that one."

"This one's different, Pol. Besides, the weather here is miserable. You wouldn't like it at all."

"I'll bring my raincoat."

"Listen, Polly, I've got an idea. I'll be finished with this story in one week, tops. Why don't we meet up afterwards and go someplace warm?"

"I'm sure there's some warm spots in London. We could go to the steam baths. They must have steam baths there, don't they? Besides, I want to go to the theatre. You can't go to the theatre on the beach!"

"The best theatre in the world is on the beach," he said.

Suddenly, he heard a rapping sound.

"Polly, there's someone at the door. I love you dearly. I'll give you a call in a couple of days, OK?"

She sighed. And then she said, rather grudgingly, "OK."

*

158

He opened up the door. It was Kate. Behind her was Ron Chancellor and another man he had never seen.

"We thought we'd meet up here," Chancellor said. "All right, Sunshine?"

Joseph nodded. "OK," he said. "But all I can offer you is tea. And I only have one tea-bag and I've been using it for days."

"Don't concern yourself," said Chancellor, pointing to his jacket pocket. "I've brought my own."

They filed throught the door. The one he hadn't seen before was a young man, gentle looking, with a long face and sad eyes. Kate and Chancellor sat down on the couch. The young man sat on a chair. Joseph sat on his desk, facing them.

"Radkin," Kate said, "this is Free."

"Hi, Free," Joseph gave him a quick salute.

"Be nice to him, Sunshine," said Chancellor. "He just got out of jail."

"Yeah?" said Joseph, inspecting the young man's face. "How was it?"

Free looked at him with his sad eyes and replied, "It was an interesting experience I'd prefer not to repeat. But I wasn't treated badly considering the other fellows there could hardly believe I'd been sent up for releasing puppies from smoking machines . . ."

"I bet," said Chancellor.

"How long did you get sent up for?" asked Joseph.

"Three years. But I got out in two, for what they call good behavior. Actually, all that means is that I went to bed on time and I didn't complain at meals — though, if you're a vegetarian, I should tell you, the food is hell."

Joseph looked at Kate. "You know him from the articles you were doing on the anti-blood sports movement, I suppose."

"That's right," said Kate. "Free knows all about the hunt."

"We'd like to disrupt the one at Foxton Manor," said Free. "Maybe we'll save an animal, maybe not. But at least we'll let the bastards know we were around . . ." He handed Joseph a leaflet.

Joseph glanced at the leaflet and then handed it back. "Not like that you won't," he said, taking from his pocket the notice he had lifted at Hughes' Hampstead house. "You got the wrong time and place. And — oh, yes — be sure to wear a white carnation."

It was after Free had left that Chancellor said, "I don't give a shit about blood sports. As far as I'm concerned it's better to shoot a fox than someone walking down the street, if you have to get it out of your system. But the Palmerston hunt is the chance to get the evidence we need. Free and his group can give us our diversion . . ."

"To do what?" asked Joseph.

"To do our own little shooting," Chancellor replied, taking three tiny cameras from his bag and giving one to Kate and one to Joseph. "Don't get caught with these," he warned, "or they'll have you for it."

Then Chancellor pulled out a rolled-up piece of paper and spread it out on the coffee-table by the couch. "Come here," he motioned to Joseph. "This is a plan of Foxton Farms."

Joseph came over and knelt down.

"The stables are to the left of the manor as you come in through the gate. At the right is another building enclosed by a fence — that's the one I'm concerned with."

"You've been there before?" asked Joseph.

"Just a few brief visits at night to reconnoiter. It's pretty well guarded. But, if Free handles it right, they'll need all their muscle to contend with the 'do-gooders'."

"I'm not so sure," said Joseph. "The hunt people think they've put 'em off the scent by changing the meeting place."

"Then someone will just have to set them straight, won't they?" Chancellor said, with a wicked little smile.

Joseph looked at Kate. He tried to meet her eye, but Kate looked down.

"We'll meet outside Kate's flat tomorrow morning at four

a.m. The drive should take about an hour. Bring all-weather gear," said Chancellor, getting up. He looked at Joseph and then pointed to the miniature camera. "And between now and then, see if you can learn how to use that."

Chapter 17

He couldn't fall asleep that night. He never could when there was a hunt the next day. Not that he had ever been on a hunt before. But he was always one for setting precedents.

About three in the morning he finally started snoring. His alarm went off a half-hour later. Grumbling like a bear forced out of hibernation, he rolled out of bed. Then, more as a way of waking up than achieving even a minor degree of sartorial splendor, he washed his face and combed his hair.

It was still dark as he stumbled out. Kate and Chancellor were waiting for him in the car. He climbed into the Mini and closed the door. Chancellor started the engine and took off.

No one said a word until they hit the motorway. Chancellor was driving like a maniac. He kept the throttle flush against the floor. He was the first one to speak.

"Good time to drive," he said, chewing on a toothpick which he pushed with his tongue from one side of his mouth to the other. "No one on the roads."

"If they were," said Joseph, huddled in his wrappings for some warmth, "we wouldn't stand a chance. Anything bigger than a rabbit hits your souped-up toy, we'd all be dead."

Chancellor laughed. It seemed to Joseph that he was in an especially good mood. "This toy, as you call it, kept England alive once upon a time. Great little car; they don't make them like this anymore."

"Small wonder," said Joseph. "In the States they don't let anything on the roads that's smaller than the person driving it."

"You bring your camera, Sunshine?" asked Chancellor, ignoring his remark.

Joseph patted his pocket. "Right here, chief."

"Why don't we go over our cover stories?" said Kate, pouring some coffee out of a thermos.

"Cover stories?" asked Joseph, turning around and looking toward the back.

"Well we can't really introduce ourselves as journalists, if someone asks, can we?" she said, putting a cup of coffee in his hand.

"I thought I'd just say I was an American tourist doing the country-manor trek."

"At five a.m?" asked Chancellor.

"I'm an early riser," said Joseph, stifling a yawn.

"You're the one with the invite, Sunshine. Tell them you're an American millionaire, director of a hunting club back home. Tell them you're a friend of Hughes . . ."

"Won't he be there?" asked Joseph.

"Not likely," Chancellor said. "He impressed me as the type who sends someone else to get his fox. Besides, there'll be swarms of people about."

"What about you?" said Joseph, turning to Kate.

"It's better that we go our separate ways," said Chancellor, answering for her. "That way we have three opportunities instead of one . . ."

"Opportunities for what?" asked Joseph.

Chancellor chewed down hard on his toothpick. "To find out what we want to know. We need someone with the hunting crowd. Neither Kate nor I would fit in with their set."

"And you mean I would?" Joseph said with justifiable surprise.

"You're the generic American, Radkin, as far as they're concerned. They have nothing except clothing and appearance to judge your class. On the other hand, they'd have us pegged as soon as we opened our mouths."

Joseph looked down at what he was wearing. "Somehow I don't think I qualify as high fashion."

Kate picked up a duffel bag from the floor and pushed it toward him. "The things you'll be needing are in here."

He gave her a look of amazement.

"By the way," said Chancellor, pointing to a box sitting on the seat between them, "there's something else for you . . ."

"Something else for me?" said Joseph. "Oh, how sweet!"

He opened it up. Inside the box was a flower — a white carnation.

They let him out on a small country road. He changed his clothes behind a tree.

"Leave the duffel bag there," said Chancellor. "Just in case we get separated. If all goes well, we'll meet back here at nine tonight."

"How did you know what size I wore?" asked Joseph, from behind his tree.

"Same size as Rose, aren't you?" said Chancellor, revving up the engine. He nodded toward the back. "Kate picked them out for you."

Having put on his costume, Joseph walked back to the car. Through the side-mirror, he caught a glimpse of Kate, sitting in the back, looking sheepish.

"You look good in pink," Chancellor said. "It suits you."

Joseph looked at the jacket and then he pulled off his hat and inspected it. "Some outfit!" He wiggled his riding stick, testing it out. "Isn't there a horse that's supposed to go along with this thing?"

"Yes," said Chancellor, revving his engine again. "But if anyone asks you, just say that it got lost."

"Sure. I'll say I lost it in a poker game. How about that?"

"You don't have far to walk," Chancellor continued, "the Hare and the Hound is just a few hundred yards along, at the crossroads."

"Good. Just enough to work up a thirst."

"And by the way, Radkin . . ."

"Yeah?"

"This is the road where your colleague's body was found. So watch out for passing trucks."

On the distant horizon, facing east, there was a glow of

morning light. Two hundred yards along, there was a bend in the road, and then, a bit further, he began to hear what sounded like a buzz from a swarm of bees. Further still, the sky becoming slightly brighter, he saw through the sparkling mist a group of horses, packed tightly together, pawing the ground. And out of the quiet of the countryside, he saw emerge a curious scene set in the parking lot of a lonely pub. Hundreds of people were gathered, some dressed in pink jackets, some dressed in black, some just in their anoraks. Some, on the periphery, drank steaming coffee from mugs. Others, were dousing themselves in a spray of morning champagne.

Working his way around the crowd, Joseph stopped by a small group of men who were passing a hot thermos full of brew from one to another. If he were forced to guess, he would have figured them to be chartered accountants or merchant bankers judging from their pale skin and the practiced look of tedium on their faces. They were a little too puffy to be sportsmen, he thought — much more the armchair kind of adventurer, who would rather read about a shoot in the pages of the *Telegraph* than have to go through all the muck.

He was hoping the thermos might find its way to him if he stood there long enough. Unfortunately, having all filled their little cups, the thermos was commandeered by the plumper of the group, a balding man with a nose as bright as a ripened cherry, who tucked it away inside a little sack after screwing on the lid.

"This is your first time, isn't it, James?" Ripe Nose said. His words were directed to a frail young man who stood opposite him, cold and gaunt.

"Yes. I'm rather looking forward to it," replied the boney one.

"Never seen the old man in action then?" asked a whiskered fellow to his right whose moustache was so stiff and straight it might have been used as a clothes-rack. He glanced in Joseph's direction as he drained his cup. Joseph licked his chapped lips and managed to restrain a sigh.

"I've studied his cases, of course," James replied, playing the foil to the elder man's smirk, "though I don't suppose he's still the man he was . . ."

"Oh, he's got a bit of fire left!" the moustached one chortled.

Joseph was just lighting up a cigarette when he felt a hand on his shoulder.

"Got a match?" someone said.

Turning, Joseph saw a man whose face was half hidden inside the hood of his anorak. It was Free. He was wearing a white carnation.

"Wouldn't think your sort would be caught dead smoking fags," Joseph said, handing him his little box of matches. "Isn't it against your religion?"

"Who said anything about fags?" Free mumbled under his breath as he pocketed the matches.

As Joseph watched Free step into the crowd and disappear, another voice rang out: "Oh, I say! Aren't you old Billy Beauchamp?"

Turning back, Joseph saw a taller man, dressed the same as him (but looking comfortable in his gear), with blond hair and rosy cheeks and a wide boyish grin. The man stuck out his hand: "It's me! Pim! You must remember! Last year. Ascot."

Before Joseph could say a word Pim was waving his hand in the air. "Bunnie! Darling! Come over here quick! Look who I found! It's Billy!"

A young woman, who could have been his twin, came over, champagne sloshing from her glass and said, "My God, Pimmy. This isn't Billy Beauchamp." Then she narrowed her eyes and, rocking gently on her toes, like a sleek yacht caught up in the wrong kind of wind, she said to Joseph, "You're not Billy, are you?"

"I'm afraid not," said Joseph.

"Yes, you are!" said Pim, looking at Joseph demandingly. "I'd know you anywhere!"

"Really! Sometimes you can be such a dodo, Pimmy, dear. Anyone with ears would know this man is American. Billy wasn't American." Bunnie took another drink of her champagne, looked at Joseph and said, "You really do have to forgive my brother, Mr . . . ?"

It slipped out before he could think. "Uh . . . Rose. Mike Rose." It was only afterwards that he realized it was a pretty stupid thing to have done.

"You really do have to forgive my brother, Mr Rose. His cord was twisted when he was born. He didn't get much oxygen to his brain."

"It was not and I did so!" Pim protested. He looked at Joseph and smiled charmingly, "Very pleased to meet you, Rose."

"Hi," said Joseph, shaking hands.

"You're not a lawyer, I hope," said Pim.

"Wouldn't dream of it," said Joseph. "Though I do like the wigs you guys wear." He looked at Pim questioningly. "Lots of lawyers here today?"

"Always," said Pim. "What is it then? Stocks and bonds?"

"More like options," Joseph replied.

"Options!" said Bunnie with some admiration. "That's rather complex, isn't it? What exactly do you do?"

"Well, for example, people often want simple options on important financial matters — things that can be answered by either 'yes' or 'no'. So they come to me for my advice."

"Give me an example," said Pim. "I'm very interested in finance."

"Financiers often want to know the answer to questions like, 'What would be the effect on Jolly-Jack Chewing Gum if it was contaminated by nuclear waste? Would they be liable for damages if kids who ate their product started coming down with radiation disease?'"

"You must have to do a dreadful amount of thinking, Michael," said Bunnie.

"'Mike'," he said. "Not really. I just ask Polly. If she says 'no' then I go back and say 'yes'. At least half the time I'm right. The other half I'm wrong. But fifty per cent is a good average . . . at least in my line of work."

"You can make a fortune on fifty per cent," said Pim.

"It depends on what fifty per cent, though," said Bunnie. "If you back the wrong fifty per cent, you can end up losing your shirt."

"I always try to keep two shirts," said Joseph. "That way, if I lose one, I still have a spare."

There was a sudden commotion across the way. Joseph noticed a small group of people holding placards had appeared and were being accosted by hunters dressed, like him, in pink.

"What's going on?" he asked.

"Hunt saboteurs," said Bunnie, with a note of disdain. "Anarchists. They can't let anyone have a good time without sticking their snotty little noses in."

In a matter of minutes the huntsmen had collected the placards and had trampled them into the ground. Most of the saboteurs had retreated into the woods. Several, however, had been caught and were being treated to a swim in a nearby pond.

"That's not very sporting, is it?" asked Joseph, feeling a sickening taste in his mouth.

"They're perfectly awful people, Michael," Bunnie hissed. "Barbarians. Actually, soaking's too good for them. They ought to be whipped!"

Joseph took the miniature camera from his pocket and, holding it surreptitiously by his side, snapped the shutter as a handsome Adonis grabbed the last placard from a scruffy young woman, broke it in half, tossed it into the pool, and then, lifting her bodily, threw her in as well.

At the same time, glancing sideways, he noticed someone familiar step out of the woods, lighting what looked like sticks of dynamite. Suddenly the fields came alive with a mighty blast. In an instant all was smoke and chaos.

"Firecrackers, damn them!" Pim shouted.

A few of the hunters rushed for their horses. But it was too late. They could only watch helplessly as the steads tore loose from their tethers and bolted madly away.

Joseph looked at Pim and could hardly restrain a smile. "Well, I guess that's it, huh? Score one for the fox, I'd say. What happens now? Everyone pack up and go home?"

Pim shook his head. "Oh, we always keep a spare just in case something like this happens . . ."

"A spare what?" asked Joseph, giving him a curious look.

Pim motioned to his right and Joseph noticed a wire cage being lifted into a truck with a furry little animal peering out.

"What's happening?" asked Joseph.

"Just a little fun," said Pim, a twinkle in his eye. "Surely you're a member of the club?"

"Yes, of course . . . lots of clubs. Which club did you have in mind?"

"The Lodge. You know — James Berry."

Chapter 18

It was a big room, large enough to hold a ball, perhaps, once upon a time, but now there was a musty smell. A small stage had been set up at the far end of the room and upon the stage was a long wooden table. Rows of seats — wooden pews, in fact — faced the stage. The seats were filled with hunters dressed in their pink jackets. Between the seats and the stage, two other tables had been set up, equidistant from a central aisle. At these tables sat men in robes and white wigs, looking very stern, like in a picture from a storybook, drawings by Tenniel.

It was a court. A court of sorts. Definitely not the Old Bailey — Joseph knew that. But it had the certain feel of authority and power, like other places where the game of justice was played out.

And standing lonely in the dock was the prisoner with four legs. Cowering in its cage, it seemed to know what lay in store. Each little noise, a laugh, a sudden cough, made it turn its furry head in a nervous jerk. And then, in a reaction of momentary defiance, like any cornered prey, it would bare its teeth and growl — only to end up cringing in its corner once again.

"This isn't a joke?" Joseph asked, turning to look at Pim.

"Of course it's not a joke," said Pim. "But it's jolly good fun! And it keeps old Palmerston in shape. Needn't worry, though. Reynard, there, will get a fair hearing and he'll cetainly have more of a chance than the poor chicken he ate!"

"Chicken?"

"Or duck or rabbit. Something like that. It doesn't, really make any difference, does it?"

"No," said Joseph. "I suppose not."

All at once, a man in full livery came in and stood on the stage. He carried a long staff which he pounded on the floor. The room came to an abrupt silence.

"Hear ye! Hear ye! James Berry's Court is now is session, Judge Palmerston presiding. All those present will be upstanding."

The audience stood up stiff and straight. Though a few whispered jocular remarks could be heard. And then . . .

"Here come de judge . . ." Joseph muttered to himself.

Palmerston, the elder, wasn't quite as tottering as Joseph had suspected. There was still a bit of spryness to the man. Perhaps, Joseph thought to himself, there was something to be said for keeping a hand in your profession after you've retired.

Adjusting his wig, the judge took his seat. And, taking their cue, so did everyone else.

The judge picked up a brief on his table, glanced at it and then, looking over at the cage, he said, "Reynard Fox, you've been accused of eating the farmer's geese. How do you plead?"

The lawyer for the defense rose. "Not guilty, your honor."

"Very well," said the judge. Nodding to the prosecutor at the table to his left, he signaled for the trial to begin.

It was, Joseph had to admit, a closely fought case. The prosecutor was quite forceful in his condemnation of the fox, speaking of the goose as a fine and honorable animal who had provided a plethora of eggs for her master, as well as bearing several healthy gaggles over the past years. The fox, he said, was cunning in its crime, waiting for precisely the proper moment to raid the nest, devouring the eggs and then grabbing the goose itself in its mouth, clamping its powerful jaws shut and breaking the poor creature's neck. The goose, of course, was defenseless. What could it do? Trying to protect her children, she went to her death so her goslings could survive. She was a martyr, he said, in a voice that had surely carried others to their doom, she was a loyal worker, a financial asset to her master, but most of all she was — a mother.

Looking around the room, Joseph saw that several hunters were forced to wipe their eyes.

171

It was now left to the defense. And it was quite a brave show, Joseph thought. The fox's lawyer really laid it on the line. A fox, he said, was a simple creature who, like us, was forced to eat to stay alive. Now, does the fox live in a society where food is provided for him? Can he go to the refrigerator when hunger strikes? Of course not, my dear gentlemen, he said. It must provide not only for itself but for its cubs. (For, yes, the fox has children, too.) If the goose was killed and eaten, it was an act of God, not a malicious stroke of evil. As humans, he insisted, we must be merciful and just. If we searched our hearts, the fox could not, in clear conscience, be convicted of a crime.

Two witnesses had been called to testify. The prosecution had brought in the farmer's wife (one of the ladies dressed up for the part). She identified the fox, by his markings, as the one who killed the goose.

The defense brought in a so-called expert in natural history (one of the hunters, naturally) to remind them that foxes in the wild look pretty much the same to the untrained eye, and that it is nearly impossible to distinguish a particular fox at a moment's glance — especially if it's in the act of killing its prey.

It was left, therefore, to the judge to make his summation. Whatever the arguments, he said, one mustn't let one's emotions hold sway. It's true that the fox was a simple creature who by nature hunts to eat. However, we are a society ruled by law. And the law is quite specific about murder in the act of theft. The fox had been identified by the farmer's wife, who in fact, had a trained eye for foxes — having chased off many in her time. (A few titters were heard.) The goose that was killed had provided for a human family — an all-important notion since a civilized society must follow the law of man and not the law of the wild. Keeping these things in mind, said the judge, taking off his glasses and rubbing his eyes, it was up to the jury to decide the fate of Reynard Fox.

The matter was dealt with quickly, without to-do. The jury,

who was the entire lodge, it seems, rose as one (except for Joseph who whispered to Pim that he had suddenly twisted his leg), when the clerk called out: "How do you decide?"

"Guilty!"

The sound echoed through the room.

"They're not serious, are they?" Joseph whispered.

"Oh, quite!" said Pim. He held his finger to his lips. "But now's the fun!"

The judge's expression grew solemn as he put the black cloth upon his head and said in sonorous tones, "Prisoner at the bar, I am no further able to treat you as being innocent of the dreadful crime laid to your charge. You have been convicted by a jury after a lengthy and most painful investigation, followed by a defense which was in every respect worthy of the case. The jury have convicted you and the law leaves to me no discretion . . ."

The sentence was read out.

"You're quite fortunate, you know," said Pim, as they followed the procession into the courtyard. "It's rare to see the entire enactment. Sometimes they're a little ragged if the dogs have got to them first."

"No trials then, I guess," said Joseph.

"Oh, we try to hold one every month. More for old Palmerston than for us, you know. But sometimes we're forced to use a pig or goat to test the apparatus . . ."

"The apparatus?" Joseph looked at him questioningly.

Pim motioned to a structure in the middle of the courtyard which was being unveiled. "Quite an antique, really," he said. "But everything is kept nicely oiled."

Joseph looked up at the gallows which had now been exposed and felt his stomach turn sour. "Try to keep it in good use, do you?" he said, hardly able to keep a trace of sarcasm from coming through.

"Well, you chaps in America are really far ahead of us," said Pim. "But I think you've really lost the aesthetic." He glanced up at the gallows admiringly. Then, looking back at

173

Joseph, he said, "We kept exactly to old Berry's specifications. The rope is made from finest Italian hemp, exactly three-quarters of an inch thickness and thirteen feet in length. The ring, through which the other end of the rope is passed to form the noose, is made of brass. And the washer which slips up behind it, is made of the finest leather. The scaffold, itself, is made of oak. The draw bars underneath the trap are of solid iron, and precision built, as both of the trapdoors need to open at the same time and suddenly so there's no rebound."

"I see," said Joseph, feeling truly ill. "How do you find your hangman?" he asked. "I assume the profession has pretty well died out."

"A terrierman usually volunteers," said Pim. He gestured toward a man ascending the scaffold. "That's one of them now."

There was almost a sense of celebration in the courtyard. People were chatting and every so often a servant would appear with a trayful of drinks. However, when the terrierman reached the top of the scaffold, all eyes were upon him as the cage was passed up.

"I hope the poor thing was at least given its last meal," Joseph said.

"Oh, he was thrown a chicken leg or two, I suspect," said Pim. "Laced with some tranquilizer, of course. Need to, you see, or else they bounce around too much."

Certainly the fox was quiet, Joseph thought, as the hangman took it from its cage and strapped what, if it were human, would have been its arms to its chest. Then a white hood was placed over the fox's head.

Lifting it now by its shoulders, the hangman placed the fox directly under the gallows beam, pinioning the hind legs just below the knees and from there suspending a lead weight.

The rope was adjusted around its neck.

The spectators fell quiet. There was a strange and eerie hush.

Then, as the hangman pulled the trapdoor bolt, there was a sudden cry from the fox as it fell. The rope jerked taut and an awful sound was heard as the backbone snapped. The head slumped forward. The hood fell off. The eyes bulged out. A few drops of blood dribbled from its mouth. And that was that.

The black flag was raised and the spectators lifted their glasses and cheered.

Joseph took his miniature camera out and snapped a shot.

"I say!" someone shouted out. "That chap's taken a picture again!"

Joseph turned around and saw the same Adonis who had thrown the woman in the pond.

The man stepped forward and grabbed the camera from Joseph's hands. "Who knows this man?" Adonis shouted.

"Why it's Rose, of course," said Pim. "He's an old boy. An options dealer from New York. He's all right."

"Rose?" someone shouted. "What's his Christian name?"

Pim scratched his head. "His Christian name is Michael, I think . . ."

"Pim, you imbecile!" Adonis yelled. "Michael Rose is dead!"

"He's not!" said Pim. "How could he be? He's standing right here next to me!"

But, in fact, he wasn't. For Joseph had taken off at the speed of light and was now racing through the gate and out into the yard.

"Must be the blackguard whose clothes we found!" someone else shouted out.

It took a moment before a group of hunters followed in hot pursuit. As Joseph, feeling like a fox, himself, dashed round a wall of shrubs, he suddenly heard someone call his name: "Radkin! Over here, quick as you can!"

Plunging into a labyrinthine maze of sculptured hedge, he saw it was Kate. She grabbed his hand and pulled him into a little hollow dug from under the thick growth of bush.

From that vantage they could see the front of the manor. The hunters were already gathering with their hounds.

"Look!" she whispered. "They have your bag of clothes!"

Sure enough, someone had come up with Joseph's duffel

bag. It was opened. The clothes were given to the dogs to get his smell.

Joseph's heart went to his throat.

"It's OK," said Kate. "I took precautions . . ."

"What'd you do?" Joseph asked. "Take out double indemnity insurance on me?"

"I laid a trail with something to keep them off the scent."

"Well, I hope it works," he said.

"It's what the French Resistance used during the war to confuse the Germans . . ."

"What's that?" he asked her.

"Cocaine," she said.

Sure enough, Kate's subterfuge had worked. The dogs had run around in circles, howling madly, until they were led away exhausted and, judging from their appearance, Joseph figured, higher than a weatherman's kite.

They waited until nightfall. When all seemed still, they snuck off, keeping close to cover, till they came to the perimeter — a stone wall some eight feet high.

Kate, far more agile than he, climbed upon his shoulders and pulled herself up. Leaning back, she grabbed his hand and gave him the leverage he needed to scale the wall. Climbing down the other side, they were off — running fast and breathless to a nearby thicket.

A flashing of lights, some voices, and a scattered bark made them once more hide their heads. After a while, hearing nothing, they followed the edge of the woods until they came within sight of the Hare and the Hound.

The parking area of the Hare and the Hound was filled with Rolls and Bentleys, just as it had been that morning. Passing by, they could hear the buzz of voices from within. They didn't stop, but kept on till they reached the crossroads.

"Ron said he'd meet us where he left you off this morning," Kate said, as they walked through the thicket alongside the road, hungry and out of breath.

"What time?" asked Joseph, stopping to lean against a tree to rest.

"Nine."

He glanced at his watch. "Eight forty-five," he said.

She pointed ahead. "Five minutes and we'll be there. Come on!" And she hurried off again.

"Wait a second," he called after her. "Let me catch my breath . . ." But she had already disappeared into the darkness.

He took a few steps in the direction she had gone before he realized that something wasn't right. He could feel it in his toes. They told him he was soon to be made into a sucker again. How soon he didn't know.

It came out of the darkness, like a panther falling on its prey. Joseph felt a burly arm tighten around his neck, shutting off his air supply, while a hand with a steel grip forced his own arm into a merciless position behind his back. Then a knee to the bony joint at the bottom of his spine brought him heavily to the ground.

In an instant, his assailant was atop him, bearing down with all his might. He wore a ski mask so Joseph couldn't see his face. Nor could he call out, as the man's hand was clutched around Joseph's throat. All he could manage was a weak hiss, like the sound of steam from a leaky radiator.

Even so, he saw it coming. Through the pain and burning in his chest, he saw the vial. But he couldn't move. He couldn't stop it. His arms were pinned to the ground by the other's knees. His mouth was being slowly forced open to suck some air as the man snapped the vial's top off with his thumb.

With his last ounce of strength Joseph made a desperate lurch. He didn't move much, but it was enough to cause the liquid to miss his mouth and, instead, hit the side of his face.

The sudden movement caught the man off balance. He heard him wheeze. And, lurching again, Joseph felt something give way. In an instant he rolled off the grassy embankment and into the road, plunging into a flood of blinding lights.

177

He heard the squeal of brakes and then the heavy sound of footsteps running away as other footsteps started to come toward him.

He couldn't see their faces, just their forms. One man grabbed him and pulled him up. Another jabbed a needle in his arm. He felt the stinging in his shoulder as they dragged him away.

As they opened the rear door of the van, he saw a car drive slowly past. He saw her sitting in the back. She turned and her eyes caught his in a look of terror.

And then he felt the earth begin to spin and something brilliant flashed inside his head. And he wondered if the music in his ears was what the angels played to sinners who would burn a thousand years.

Chapter 19

He opened his eyes. The sky was blue. A graceful white bird was flying past. It hung a moment in the air, as if to defy every law on the books, and then swooped down again.

He was lying on a divan made of soft, pliable leather near a translucent wall, somewhere in the clouds. The room was large and well furnished with chrome and polished wood and, everywhere, glass, bright and light as crystal.

Turning over, he saw the table near him was loaded with food and drink. Fragrant coffee was brewing on a hot plate. There were dishes of cheeses, smoked salmon, caviar and breads. He rubbed his eyes and said, "This can't be hell!"

"Good morning, Mr Radkin!" came a cheerful voice. "We hope you slept well!"

He looked up. A sleek, well-dressed woman was standing by the door holding an armful of documents.

"Please help yourself to some breakfast," she said. "If you'd like a newspaper, we have the *Financial Times* — that's all, I'm afraid. But we also have *The Economist* and some specialty magazines . . ."

"Actually," said Joseph. "I'd like to take a leak."

"There is a toilet as well as a bath," she said, without skipping as much as a beat. She pointed at a door to her left.

Joseph sat up and brushed back his hair. "You wouldn't care to tell me where I am," he said, looking out into the sky. "I guess this isn't the morning flight of Concorde, is it?"

"You're in Hughes Towers," she said. "Mr Hughes asked me to buzz him when you awoke. It's ten o'clock now. Could you be ready in half an hour?"

"Ready for what? Lessons in wingless flying?" he asked, watching a minuscule cloud float by.

She gave him a tiny smile. "Have a good breakfast, Mr Radkin. I'll fetch you at half-ten." Then she made her exit, closing the door behind.

He knew it was useless, but, anyway, he got up, walked over and tried opening the door she had just closed. Sure enough, it was locked. Figuring nothing was lost, he went to the toilet and then splashed some water on his face at the sink. He looked at himself in the mirror and was surprised to find that he was still in his hunting togs.

There were some clean clothes sitting on a little table by the bath. He picked up a shirt and realized it was his own — though it had never been ironed as neatly before (if it had ever been ironed at all, that is).

He took a quick wash and changed. Then he went back to the divan, sat down, and made himself a sandwich of smoked salmon laced with caviar. He poured some coffee, settled himself comfortably on the couch, picked up the morning's issue of the *Financial Times*, took an enormous bite out of his sandwich and read that the wheat crop in Mongolia didn't do badly this year, not badly at all.

At ten twenty-five on the dot there was a perfunctory knock on the door and Miss Waxed and Polished walked back in.

"Are you ready, Mr Radkin?" she asked.

"That's always a relative question, isn't it?" he replied. "If you're asking if I'm ready for some explanation, the answer's 'yes'. But if you mean am I ready to meet God, I'd have to reply that I'd prefer to do so on my own terms."

She was waiting for him by the door. "We have some expert attorneys here, Mr Radkin. I'm sure they can arrange a meeting with whomever you wish."

He got up and stretched. "In that case, I wouldn't want to keep God waiting." He walked over to where she was standing, still carrying his cup. "Mind if I bring this along? I haven't finished yet."

She led him into a short hallway and then into a tiny room, furnished simply with drapes and a rug. Closing the door, she pressed a button. He had just put the cup to his lips when suddenly they ascended even further into the heavens.

"I wasn't expecting that," he said, as the contents of the cup splattered in his face, dripping down onto his clothes.

"Sorry, Mr Radkin. I thought you knew it was the lift," she said.

He shrugged. "Great coffee, though, where'd you get it?"

"Oh, we have our own plantations. The beans at the top of the mountains are flown directly to us. Of course, they're the best."

"Same with the salmon? Have your own rivers and oceans, as well?"

She smiled again and he saw her shining teeth. "I wouldn't doubt it, Mr Radkin. We try very hard to diversify."

"Speaking of diversity. You wouldn't know where my friend is, I don't suppose?" he said. "You didn't turn her into caviar, by any chance?"

"All our caviar comes from Russia, Mr Radkin," she said, as the little upholstered room suddenly came to a stop. "Your friend isn't Russian, is she?"

"Not unless Russia is part of Ireland now," said Joseph, following her out. "But you never know about those things, do you? I mean, the world is changing fast."

She walked quickly down a narrow hall and stopped in front of a connecting door. Checking her watch and waiting for the seconds to tick by till it was ten-thirty precisely, she gave a little rap and turning back to Joseph, said, "You can go straight in, Mr Radkin. He'll see you at once."

There was the feel of vastness and of power, like a planetarium built into a war-room of the Pentagon. A huge oak desk filled up the entire width. On the desk there was a terracotta statuette of a naked woman with her mouth open, arms uplifted, in a gesture which Joseph took as supplication. At the far end of the room, by the wall of glass, stood a figure looking down at the city below. His back was turned as Joseph came in, so he couldn't see his face.

181

"It's a great city down there, don't you agree?"

"Yeah," said Joseph. "From this perspective, I guess it is. Maybe not so great though if you're looking at it from a cardboard box underneath Hungerford Bridge."

"Sit down, Mr Radkin," he said. There was a chair at the end of the room where Joseph had come in. He pulled it slightly closer toward the desk and sat.

Hughes turned around. With the back light from the windows, he appeared in silhouette. Taking a fat cigar from a box sitting on the table, Hughes struck a match and lit it up. Then sucking in the smoke he held it in his lungs for what seemed like a minute, finally letting it out in an enormous cloudburst. "They tell me you have a curious sense of humor," he said.

"Who tells you that, Mr Hughes?"

"People whom I trust."

"The question is, do they trust you?"

"They trust me as long as I pay their bills, Mr Radkin. And I pay them well for their loyalty. Money is our bond, sir. Money, pure and simple. No other relationship exists that has any value."

"How about a little thing called 'love'?" asked Joseph. "Or am I being trite?"

Hughes took his cigar from his mouth and let out an explosive laugh. "That's a word better used by women and children, Mr Radkin. Not by a mature adult."

"Better not let Polly hear you say that," he replied, taking a final sip of coffee from the cup he had brought with him.

Hughes pulled a folder from a pile on his desk and opened it up. "'Polly . . .'" He ran his finger down a sheet. Putting it back down, he said, "Yes, I see. Your wife . . ."

"How about my dog? You know her name as well?"

Hughes picked up the sheet again. "You haven't got a dog," he said, putting it back down. "But I didn't bring you here to play games, sir."

"No?" Joseph raised his eyebrows. "Why did you bring me here, then?"

"To speak with you as a gentleman," he said. "You've entered into something you know nothing about . . ."

"Is that what happened to Mike?" Joseph cut in.

"Not quite . . ."

"Can I ask you a question, Mr Hughes?"

"If you make it brief and precise."

"Why did you have your own stepson bumped off?"

"My stepson, as you call him, was no concern of mine. But I have easier, less messy, and more effective ways of dealing with people who annoy me than murder."

"Unless, I suppose, they persist in not doing what you ask."

"That, Mr Radkin, is why several floors of this tower are inhabited by lawyers. The finest lawyers in the world who know the finest judges."

"Judges like old man Palmerston?"

Hughes bit down hard on his cigar. "Judge Palmerston is retired."

"Semi-retired, I would say," Joseph put in.

Taking the little statue of the naked woman by the neck, he flicked the ash of his cigar into her open mouth. Setting it back down, he said, "Which brings me to the reason for our meeting, Mr Radkin."

"And what is that?"

Hughes leaned forward, his hands flush on the desk. Joseph could finally see his face and he didn't like what he saw. "The Palmerston family is very dear to me. I wouldn't want them to come to any embarrassment."

"If money is the basis of all relationships, then, I suppose, in your terms 'dear' must mean expensive . . ."

Hughes straightened himself and once more receded into the bright light. "Friendship exists, Mr Radkin, amongst men who view the world in a similar fashion. But, again, that's not the point. What you saw was of no importance, a minor peccadillo, a little detail that, in fact, could blemish an otherwise pristine career."

Joseph rubbed the bristle on his cheek. "Are we talking here of Palmerston, father, or Palmerston, son?"

"Both. The sins of the father carry down to the son."

"Look, I won't argue with you about their obscene little club, Mr Hughes. I won't bore you with my own moral problems about the perversity of English justice in the hands of characters like Palmerston. Anyway, there seem to be historical precedents. But I'll lay it on the line. I think there's been a conspiracy to misdirect attention from the James Berry Memorial Lodge and the activities of a former High Court Judge and a future Tory minister — a conspiracy that's led to several deaths and an innocent young woman rotting in jail."

A thick cloud of smoke emanated from the Hughes cigar. "What do you think happened, Mr Radkin? Perhaps you could enlighten me."

"Correct me if I'm wrong, Hughes. But I suspect you know yourself. Stephen Fry got wind of the little escapades at Foxton Manor, right? He was desperate for some dough. So what's some blackmail between friends? The problem is that blackmailers can never get enough. So he was bumped off by putting a little fox poison in his coke and Lavinia was made the patsy."

"What about my stepson, Mr Radkin? How does he fit in?"

"He found out about what happened, so naturally he was . . ." Joseph suddenly stopped.

"And that's why you're still alive, is it?" asked Hughes, staring down at him.

"Maybe I'm not," said Joseph, looking out into the beautiful sunlit sky. He rubbed his arm. "What was in that syringe your men shot into me?"

"Just a simple tranquilizer. The same that's used to transport horses. You were a bit agitated, I'm told. I trust you had a good sleep."

"Oh, I slept fine. Just like a newborn colt."

"For a clever journalist, Mr Radkin, you're easily led by the nose," said Hughes.

"Most of us are," Joseph replied. "I guess that's why the press is tolerated in both our countries."

Hughes pressed a button on his desk and suddenly solid

walls came down from the ceiling and up from the floor, completely enclosing the glass. Everything went dark.

"Christ on a crutch!" Joseph said. "We're not going up again, are we?"

"You can start now, James," Hughes said in an amplified voice. A brilliant light shone from a slot in the back wall, projecting itself onto the front.

The slide was of a uniformed policeman. It was a man Joseph knew well — or so he thought.

"Inspector Ronald Hogarth Chancellor, Manchester police," said Hughes. "You recognize him, of course."

"Hogarth, you say? Pretty fancy name for a cop. He looks a little different now," said Joseph. "Less hair . . ."

"This was taken ten years ago. Right before his hearing took place."

"What hearing is that?" asked Joseph.

"An internal hearing. His wife had died, you see. The doctor who examined her suspected she might have been poisoned."

Another slide flashed on the wall.

"This is the committee's report. The evidence, they felt, was insufficient to hold a trial. But Chancellor was advised to resign which, as you can see from the next slide, he did on October 12th.

"There was also a psychiatric report," said Hughes, as a new slide flashed on the wall. "It indicated patterns of schizophrenic paranoia."

"That could mean anything," Joseph replied. "I bet half the owners of tall towers could be classified as that."

"Perhaps you're right, Mr Radkin. Not every psychiatric ailment is a debilitating disease. Some help you earn money, some help you create. But there's a few that mark a man for murder."

Another slide flashed against the wall. Joseph recognized it as the purchase order for strychnine made out to Foxton Farms. "This came from a strip of film," Hughes said. "Perhaps you've come across it . . ."

"I might have," Joseph replied.

185

"The purchase order is from one of our firms, so I know something about the way these things are written up."

"So what?" said Joseph. "The only thing I'm interested in is that there was enough strychnine available at Palmerston's ranch to kill an army."

"That very well could be," said Hughes. "Strychnine is still the most effective poison for killing farmyard pests. However, this particular purchase order has been forged."

"How do you know?"

"By the purchase-order number. In our records that particular number refers to something else."

"What are you suggesting, Hughes?" asked Joseph, looking at him suspiciously. "Why would anybody go to the trouble of forging a purchase order for stuff that would have more than likely been there anyhow?"

"To lead someone along a certain trail, Mr Radkin. Someone wanted first Michael and then you to believe Palmerston had access to strychnine and could very well have used it to kill Fry."

"And that someone, I suppose you mean, is Chancellor. You think he wanted to set up Palmerston just to clear his daughter?"

"I'm convinced Ronald Chancellor, himself, killed Fry. And so, in fact, was Michael . . ."

Joseph's jaw dropped about an inch and a half. "Mike? He told you this?"

"Michael had a meeting with me the morning of the day he died. He told me of his suspicions and showed me his documentation."

"Why? You two didn't get along that well, I understand."

"You understand correctly, Mr Radkin. But Michael wasn't opposed to asking for my help when he needed it."

"If you were convinced Chancellor was a killer, how come the police haven't arrested him?"

"Because we haven't any real evidence yet, Mr Radkin. None that would stand up in court, that is."

Joseph squinted his eyes to try to make out the expression on his face. "Why would Chancellor have killed Fry?"

"Psychotics can also love their daughters. Fry was a bad egg. Chancellor had tried to get his daughter to leave him several times, which, in fact, she did — unfortunately, only to return. What actually brought him to decide to murder Fry, I wouldn't know. Perhaps Fry actually did try to blackmail Palmerston and Chancellor found out about it. Maybe he saw it as an opportunity to get rid of Fry by putting the blame on an innocent man who could have had a motive. It backfired, of course, as the prime suspect became the daughter . . ."

"There was the chemist who swore she tried to buy strychnine from him. How do you explain that?"

"Perhaps she did. Maybe Chancellor put her up to it."

"There was a letter from a woman who claims she was hired by someone to ask for the stuff. Her body was found decomposing in the Thames."

"Chancellor could well have hired her to cover his tracks. Then he killed her to shut her up."

Hughes pushed a button. The walls receded into the floor and ceiling again. The room opened up to the sky. The light was very bright.

Joseph rubbed his eyes and looked over at Hughes' silhouette. "You have an answer for everything. Your type usually does, I guess."

"That's why my type lives in luxury, Mr Radkin. And your type lives in . . ."

"Shit?"

"If you insist," Hughes said. "But I'd urge you very strongly to take precautions. Your friend Chancellor knows his time is almost up. When an animal is cornered, it turns very mean. Chancellor has killed several times already. He's got the taste of blood."

Joseph stood up. "What have you done with Kate, Mr Hughes?"

"I've done nothing with her or anyone else. Your friend

was simply cautioned not to trespass on private property. She was subsequently given a ride back to her house."

"Well," said Joseph, lifting his cup, "thanks for the coffee and the nap. I'd like to chat longer but I have an appointment with my hairdresser and you know how they can get. So, if you could call the bailiff . . ."

"You're not a prisoner, Mr Radkin. You're free to go any time you wish." And saying that, Hughes sat down at his desk and started going through some papers as if Joseph had now ceased to exist.

"I'll say 'cheerio' then." Joseph started walking toward the door. Suddenly, he turned around again.

"Oh, one other thing. Who's Dr Singh, Mr Hughes? And why did he go back to India?"

Hughes looked up. A shadow was cast upon his face. His voice was like an icicle. "One more word of advice, Mr Radkin . . ."

"Lots of free advice. Must be my luck day," said Joseph.

"Some people pay millions for my advice," said Hughes. "Some fail to listen. They only have themselves to blame when things don't work out for them."

"I'm all ears," he said, putting his finger behind a lobe.

Hughes pointed his burning cigar in Joseph's direction. "Take care what you write. I notice from your file that you've been hit by a libel suit before."

"I only write what's fit to print," he said.

"Most journalists would say that, I suspect. My lawyers have to teach them there's often a narrow line between what is fit and what's not. One toe over that line and their career could come to a very abrupt and expensive demise."

Joseph turned and pointed to a door to the left of the one he came in. "That the exit or the fast chute to the cellar?"

"It's the express elevator to the parking garage," Hughes said, as he started going through his papers again. "You can use it as a way out."

Joseph reached for the door knob and then turned around once more. "You know, Hughes, I don't like you. And I don't like what you stand for. Maybe I'm just a hack writer with a wife and kids and a drawer full of bills waiting to be paid, but I wouldn't trade my life for your little piece of sky — even if the clouds are loaded with caviar and champagne!"

Hughes looked up from his desk again and took a puff on his cigar. He grinned, like a wolf who truly enjoyed eating grandmothers for lunch, and said, "Those are brave words, Mr Radkin. I hope you don't live to regret them some day."

It took about ten seconds to drop twenty floors. At least that's what Joseph's stomach thought when it reached the bottom.

The parking garage where he emerged was dimly lit — compared to the brilliance from up above — and reeked of motor fumes and axle grease. To his left was a ramp which led up to the street. Joseph stood for a moment, his hands in his pockets, and then he turned right.

He walked along the drive into the bowels of the garage until he came to a separate parking bay. There was a grease rack and a petrol pump and a little room for the chauffeurs to stay.

And there he saw it, like an ancient leopard, gleaming bright. A valet was polishing it under a light: the black limousine with mirrored windows he had seen the other day.

Chapter 20

From the pristine office in the stars he was catapulted back into the world of slime. The traffic, the noise, the litter, the rush, the spittle on the pavement, the puke in the gutter — that was his home. Not up above in that watchtower for the rich. Here at least he could breathe. The air might not be pure, he thought, pretty polluted, in fact; but at least there weren't any pretentious filtration systems that ended up giving you Legionnaire's Disease.

He took a taxi to Rona Road. After the cabby dropped him off, he walked over to Kate's place and gave a knock. Nobody replied. He stood there a moment and then knocked again. He put his ear against the door and, hearing nothing, went over to the window and tried to peer inside. The drapes were pulled slightly back so he could get a partial view. From what he could see, the place was a wreck. But, as Kate said, it was usually that way.

He rang the upstairs bell to see if the neighbors were in. They weren't. Or they weren't answering.

Hands in his pocket, he crossed the street. He was about to open the front door of his house when he heard a telltale sound. He opened the door and walked inside. There she was, kerchief wrapped around her head, cheerfully hoovering away.

"Hello, Mrs White," he said. "How's the Emerald Isle? I heard your vacuum cleaner crying so I fed it some dust. Hope that's OK."

"We had a grand time, Mr Radkin. It's a beautiful country, so green and clean and friendly."

He rubbed the bristles on his cheek and said, "Sounds great. Any messages while I was out getting bumped on the head?"

190

"Miss O'Malley came by," she said.

"You mean Kate?"

She gave him a look of disapproval. "Yes. She seemed quite distressed."

"Did she leave a note?"

"It's on the table over there," she said, pointing at the little marble thing standing lonely by the wall.

He went over and picked it up.

"You did say you're a married man, Mr Radkin?"

"That's right. Happily married. Two kids. Cottage. White picket fence. Church. Pot-roast on Sunday. Never look at other women unless they look at me first. Kate's just a friend . . ."

The envelope was open. He figured it already had been read: "Radkin: Bloody Hell! Where the blazes are you? I've been ringing every ten minutes. What happened to you last night? I have to get out of the house before I go insane. If you get back before me, I'll be at the Everyman — up in Hampstead. Hope to God you're all right! Love, Kate."

He looked back at Mrs White. "When did Kate leave this off?" he asked.

"Not more than a quarter of an hour ago," she said, starting up her dust-eating machine again. "There was also another letter that came earlier today. I put it underneath your door."

The letter was from Virginia Hughes and had been sent by special messenger. It was a short note: "I'm sorry about what happened the other day. Please give me a ring at your convenience. I'll be at home today." At the bottom she had written in her personal telephone number.

He lit up a cigarette and placed the call. She answered on the second ring: "Hello?"

"Mrs Hughes? This is Joseph Radkin."

"Oh, Mr Radkin. I'm glad you called. I wanted to apologize about the other day. I'm sorry I wasn't able to receive you."

"Your butler forwarded your apologies."

191

"Yes, I'm sure he did," she said with a trace of sarcasm. "Mr Radkin, I hope you don't judge me too harshly. There's a great deal you don't know . . ."

"You're telling me!"

"My husband and I don't see eye to eye on many things . . ."

"Like the death of your son?"

There was a brief hesitation and then she said, "Perhaps."

"Look," he said, "I know this is difficult for you. But, frankly, I'm fed up. I've been beaten, drugged and forced to see things that I'd rather not. I think it's time we stopped waltzing around. If you got something to say, lady, just spit it out. And while you're at it, maybe you could tell me about the guy whose card you're handing round."

"All right," she said. "About a week before his death Michael was having a drink with me at the house. My husband and Michael didn't get along, so sometimes it was a bit awkward, you understand . . ."

"I know that. And believe me, I do understand."

"My husband had a meeting that afternoon in his study with a man from one of his firms."

"Which firm was that?"

"His pharmaceutical firm. I believe he was involved in some important research project."

Joseph took his pencil and started scribbling notes. "Go on."

"This man and my husband had got into a dreadful quarrel . . ."

"How close is your husband's study from where you entertained your son?"

"On the other side of the house. But their quarrel was very loud and the doors and windows were open."

"I see."

"A while later the man came downstairs. He waited in the hallway adjoining the sitting-room where Michael and I were having drinks. The door to the hallway was open. I could see he was very upset . . ."

192

"I imagine many people who meet with your husband become very upset, Mrs Hughes."

"He waited there a moment, as if he wasn't sure if he should leave. I went out to see if I could talk to him."

"Why?"

"Well, he seemed so upset, you see . . ."

"That was very kind of you. Go on."

"He told me that my husband had become so angry that he kicked him out before he had a chance to present his case. He gave me his card and begged me to give it to my husband when he calmed down."

"But if he was employed by your husband, then surely Mr Hughes knew where to reach him," Joseph said.

Her voice sounded just a little flustered. "Of course, but the records were at the office and he wanted my husband to be able to reach him that night."

"So he gave you his card to give to your husband."

"That's right."

"And you gave his card to Mike?"

"Michael wanted to know what was going on. You see, he didn't like my husband . . ."

"And you gave Mike the card? Just like that?"

"He insisted."

"Pardon my language, Mrs Hughes, but this all sounds like a load of crap! I knew Mike. He was a professional journalist, not an amateur comedian. He wouldn't waste his time following up something because he heard what sounded like an argument. Besides, I've seen your mansion. It's built better than most shacks. I don't think you could have heard anything half a house away!"

"You're a very insolent man, Mr Radkin!" she said.

"Of course I'm insolent!" he shot back. "How do you think I've been able to last in this business? But my insolence, or lack of it, isn't the point."

"What is the point?" she asked, coldly.

"The point is you giving me this information. I'm asking myself 'why'?"

193

"Because you wanted to find out about my son."

"Yes, that's right. I understand about my motives. I'm not so sure about yours."

"My motives aren't so hard to understand." Her voice broke slightly. I am . . . I was . . . his mother."

"I realize that. I'm sure in your own way, you loved your son very much. But you know what I think? I think you wanted to stick the knife into your husband. I've met him, Mrs Hughes. Any man who gets his kicks by putting his ashes into a naked lady's mouth must be a pretty detestable guy. I think that you tried to set him up and in the process made use of your son. I'm not sure how or what you did, or how this Dr Singh fits in. But you're the one who gave Mike the information. You told him of some shenanigan that was going on — something you overheard. And you told him because you knew it would interest him. What you didn't count on is how it ended up!"

He heard a click on the other end of the line.

"Hello? Mrs Hughes? Are you there?"

She wasn't. The line was dead.

The Everyman was nearly empty as he pushed open the swinging doors. The music had changed to Billie Holiday — but she was still sitting at the bar, nursing a Becks, looking like the origin of the Blues itself.

She didn't see him as he walked up to where she sat.

"Hi, babe," he said.

She jumped down from the stool and gave him a hug and a kiss. "Radkin! God, it's good to see you! I thought you were dead!"

"I told you I had an unbreakable head. What happened to you, Kate?"

"They turned me over to the cops. Said I was found molesting the sheep or something. The jail was full of anti-hunt people — some of them in pretty bad shape. Worse than me, at any rate." She looked up at him. "I was bloody scared about you, though."

194

He ordered a beer, and they walked over to a booth and sat down. "How about Chancellor?" he asked.

She shook her head. "I've been trying to call. Nobody answers at his end." She gave him a troubled look again. "What happened to you?"

He took out his cigarettes and handed her one. He lit his up and leaned forward to light hers up as well. "Someone jumped me in the woods — tried to make me drink something from a vial . . ."

"Do you know who it was?"

"I think so. But he was wearing a hood. Anyway, he was scared off by Hughes' guys. They dosed me with some sort of sleeper. I woke up in the clouds — literally. Hughes Towers. Had a meeting with the big guy himself. He tried to convince me that Chancellor killed Fry and then forged evidence that made it seem like Palmerston was the one who did it."

She looked at him hard. "Did he convince you?"

Joseph took a long drag at his smoke and then let it curl out of his mouth. "He made a pretty good case."

"And you fell for it?"

Taking a swig of beer, he looked at her through the glass. She didn't seem pleased. He put down his beer. "Did Chancellor ever say anything to you about his wife?" he asked her.

She shook her head.

"He was accused of poisoning her."

"Is that what Hughes said?"

"He showed me the report."

"Look, Radkin," she said, "you're supposed to be a hard-boiled newspaperman, not a mouthpiece for Hughes Industries!"

He took offense to that. "I'm not a mouthpiece for anyone, O'Malley, except myself. But there are some things you might try shoving through your thick skull. Chancellor tried to manipulate both of us . . ."

"So what? No one was doing him any favors! His kid's in jail!"

"A lot of other fathers' kids are there too!"

"Except his kid is innocent!"

"You don't think the jails are full of innocent kids? Come off it, Kate!"

She got up from her seat, boiling mad. "I know him better than you do!" she said. "Ron Chancellor is more of a man than you could ever hope to be! But I've seen his gentle side, Radkin. And if he's a killer, I'll eat my umbrella — and maybe your mangy mackintosh as well!"

And with that she stomped off.

"Hey!" he called after her. "Where you going?"

"Bugger off!" she shouted as she slammed through the door.

The waiter came over with another beer. "Here," he said. "It's on the house. I've had them walk out on me before."

Joseph looked up at him. The guy had sympathetic eyes. He figured it was useless to explain. Besides, what would he say? So he settled for a nod and a "thanks".

He was half-way through his beer when it struck him. He grabbed his raincoat, threw some money on the table and raced out the door.

He didn't have an address. All he remembered Chancellor said when he told him where he lived was "Burghley Road, Tufnell Park".

"Where would you like me to let you out?" the cabby asked him as he reached the corner.

"Right here will be fine," said Joseph, tossing him a bill and then jumping out.

"Oi! Don't you want your change?"

"Keep it!" Joseph shouted, jogging down the street. He couldn't remember what he gave the driver. It could have been five. It could have been fifty. But it didn't matter. He had more important things on his mind.

He reached the third crossing of Burghley Road when he saw the red Mini parked by the side, under a tree. He stopped and leaned up against it to catch his breath.

Glancing around, he suddenly realized the problem. Most of the old red-brick houses had been converted into flats. Parking wasn't easy here. Chancellor could have left his car a few corners away from his own. There were a hundred possible places he could live.

He tried the door opposite to the car, on the same side of the street. An elderly-looking woman answered. She opened it part-way and looked at him suspiciously.

"Yes?"

"I'm looking for a man named Chancellor, Ronald Chancellor. He lives somewhere on this street . . ."

"He doesn't live here," said the woman, starting to close the door.

"I know that." Joseph pointed to the red Mini. "That's his car. He's a tall man, in his fifties, thin, very lean. He's got a granddaughter who sometimes visits him — she's maybe four or five. Doesn't often speak . . ."

"I've lived here for fifty years," said the woman. "I've never seen that car. I can't say I've seen the man." She shut the door. He heard her voice continue from the inside. "And if you don't go away right now, I shall call the police!"

He tried several other doors. The answer was the same, though no one else threatened to call the cops.

"Nobody sees nothing here," he said to himself, leaning back against the car. "A great place to have a party."

He was running his hand through his hair, trying to consider what his next move would be, when he saw a young postman doing his rounds a few houses up the road.

"Hey!" he called out. "You there!"

The postman looked over at Joseph and then pointed to himself with a questioning look on his face.

"Yes, you!" Joseph ran up to him.

The young man looked slightly terrified. "I'm a postman," he said, holding out his bag. "I work for the government."

"Yeah, well that's your problem," said Radkin. "I'm looking for a man who lives on this block. His name's Chancellor. First name Ron. You know where he lives?"

197

"I'm new," said the young man. "This is the first time I've done this route."

Joseph pointed to the stack of letters the man had in his hand. "Well, look through those and see if you find one for him. OK?"

The young man shook his head. "I'm not allowed."

"All right, I'll do it then!" Joseph said, grabbing the stack of letters and rifling through them. Finding nothing, he handed the letters back to the kid.

"You can get five years for doing that!" the young man shouted, waving his finger at him.

"Oh, piss off!" said Joseph.

The postman continued his rounds, mumbling to himself. Joseph went back to lean against the Mini. He rubbed his shoulder against the door, turned around and kicked the tire. And then, like a bolt out of the blue, it suddenly struck him. He put his nose against the driver's window and tried peering in. There were all kinds of papers inside, sticking out of the glove compartment, on the seats, on the floor.

He tried the doors. They were locked. He tried shaking and kicking them. That didn't help. He stared at the doors for a moment. Cursing, he bent down and searched the ground for a well-shaped rock. Finding a good one, he straightened up, positioned it in his hand and, with one swift blow, smashed through the glass.

His hand was bleeding as he drew it back through the shattered window. He looked around. The woman who had threatened to call the police was peering out at him through the safety of her double-glazing.

He grunted something in her direction and then opened the Mini. He leaned inside and rifled the papers until he found the envelope he wanted. He noted the number and then pulled himself back out, slamming the door.

Chancellor s place was only a hundred yards away. He ran down the street till he came close. And then he saw something curious. It was parked in the shadows. A black limousine with windows of one-way glass.

He stopped short and changed course, walking up to it. The limo's engine started up.

"Hey!" Joseph shouted. He banged on the door. "Open the fuck up! I want to talk to you!"

The limo pulled away from the curb and drove off.

Joseph watched it drive slowly down the road. Turning back, he ran over to Chancellor's address.

It wasn't a place you'd bring your maiden aunt. The garden was overgrown and full of trash. The house was bleak and dark. There was the smell of rot as he opened the door that led to the entry hall.

The buzzers to the rooms were useless, he could see that. The row of buttons had been pulled half-way out so the twisted wires were exposed. They may have been connected to the current, but, even so, they weren't marked.

He looked around. The house had been carved up into countless rooms — each one drearier than the next if the hallway was anything to go by. The walls were stained with water marks and the paper was hanging down in jagged strips.

It was a place for immigrants, Joseph thought.

A thin black man with a stubbly face was coming down the stairs. He saw Joseph and he stopped. He cracked the knuckles of his hands.

"I'm looking for Chancellor," Joseph said.

The man stared at him uncomprehendingly.

"White man. Fifties. Pretty fit. Used to be a cop."

"Do a little kid sometime come visit him?"

"Yeah. What room's he in?"

The man pointed with a finger that was out of joint. "Second door down. Back of the house." Then he continued down the stairs. "Bad place for a kid," he said. "Bad place for anyone — especially someone who used to be a cop."

Joseph continued on down the cluttered hall. In the background he could hear somebody puking up. He heard a toilet flush and someone shout, "Bloody hell! Shut up!"

He knocked at the door — the second one down. There wasn't any reply.

199

"Chancellor!" he shouted. "Chancellor! I know you're there!"

He pounded his fist on the door. Then he tried the knob. It turned. The door opened up. He kicked away some laundry and walked inside.

It was dark. There was a stench — something that made his sinuses fill up. He felt his way to the window and drew open the curtain to get some light. It was stuck. He tugged at it and heard it rip.

A ray of light beamed in, working its way through the dusty room. His eyes followed the path.

And then he saw. The feeling was like a jagged knife had plunged into his chest.

Chancellor was slumped backward in a chair, his fingers frozen round a gun. Joseph wasn't going to take a second look, but it seemed to him there was nothing left of Chancellor's head.

"Don't turn on the lights," he heard her say. The voice was soft and pleading.

He turned. He could barely make out her form. She was huddled in the corner on the floor.

He went over to where she was and sat down by her side.

She buried her head between his shoulders and his chest. He could feel her face was hot.

"Did you see?" he whispered.

"No," she whispered back. "He was dead when I came in."

She was quiet. Her breathing was shallow but regular. It seemed to him she was calm. Too calm.

"I'm going to turn on the light," he said, starting to get up.

She clutched his hand. "Don't turn on the light!"

"OK, Kate. I won't." He was standing now, still holding her hand. He pulled her up. "Let's get out of here!" he said.

When they got outside, into the air, Kate sat down on the front porch. She put her head in her hands and said, "I can't go on."

Joseph stood next to her. She looked drained of any emotion. It was like the life had been sucked from her body by a giant leech.

"We have to go, Kate," he said.

She shook her head. "I can't."

He took out his pack of cigarettes and tried offering one to her. She shook her head again.

He lit up and leaned against the wall. He smoked the cigarette and when it was finished, he let the stub drop and ground it out with the heel of his shoe. Then he turned and went back inside the house.

The door to Chancellor's room was still open. The floor by the body was wet with something sticky. He went in and came up close. He held his breath so as not to smell the stench and ran his hands over the pocket of Chancellor's jacket. They weren't there. He tried the pocket of his trousers, emptying them onto the floor. Coins and bits of paper fell out. And something else. He looked down and saw what he was looking for laying in a pool of blood.

He took his handkerchief and retrieved them. Then, quickly, he went out of the room, gasping for air.

He found a communal toilet on the second floor and washed them in the sink. He felt the nausea in his stomach grow intense. He turned and threw up. It helped, but not much. He flushed the toilet and heard someone shout, "Bloody hell! Can't you shut up!"

He went outside again. She was still sitting there, comatose, her head in her hands.

"Stay there, Kate," he said, "I'll be right back."

He ran to where the Mini was parked and stuck his hand through the smashed window and opened the door. He got in and took the keys he had gotten from Chancellor's pocket and found one that fit the ignition. He started up and drove back to Chancellor's block.

He did a U-turn and drove the Mini up onto the pavement. He stuck his head out the window and pressed his hand down on the horn. He shouted, "Come on, Kate!"

She stared at him uncomprehendingly.

"Come on!" he shouted again.

She got up and walked slowly over to the car. He opened the passenger door and she got in.

He revved the engine and sped away.

Chapter 21

They were in a pub near Gospel Oak. Kate had finished one whisky and Joseph had gotten her another while he went to make his phone call. When he returned she had finished that one as well.

"Did you phone the police?" she asked.

"Why should I? They already know."

"Who told them?"

He looked into her eyes. They no longer had any fire — not like they once had. "Kate, did you see a black limousine parked in front of his house when you got there?"

"I don't recall seeing one. But I was worried. I sensed something was wrong. There could have been one. Why?"

"I saw it when I came. It was just pulling away. I saw the same car before — several times, in fact."

"Where?"

"Once in the parking garage at Hughes Towers . . ."

She held out her hand. "Give me a cigarette," she said.

He handed her one, struck a match and leaned over to light her up. She inhaled and let the smoke drift slowly from her mouth as a tear rolled down from an eye.

"Were you having an affair with him?" he asked.

"Briefly," she said. She let out an ironic laugh. "They all seem to end up dead, don't they?" She looked at him. Another tear rolled from the same eye.

"You want to give up?" he asked.

She took another drag on her cigarette and shook her head. "No. Do you?"

"Nah," he said. "Once I'm in this deep I gotta go on. I'm a sucker for stuff like that. You want me to take you home?"

"No."

"From here on in it's a dangerous game," he said, looking at her seriously. "No joke."

"I know," she said.

"You've got a kid,"

"You've got two."

"OK," he said, getting up from his chair. "Let's go."

They were driving up Hampstead hill when she said to him, "That phone call you made back in the pub, who was it to?"

"A friend of mine who's doing a little research for me," he replied. "There was a name being bandied about — a Dr Singh. It seems he once worked for the pharmaceutical wing of Hughes Industries. My friend found out that Singh had filed a suit against them that was suddenly dropped . . ."

"What was it about?"

"McIssacs couldn't find out. Seems everyone's clammed up."

"I don't understand. So somebody's upset at Hughes and files a suit. What does it have to do with us?"

"Kate, Singh was the mystery man Mike was looking for! His mother knew Singh was threatening Hughes with something. It must have been pretty brutal. Anyway, she tipped him off . . ."

"That was his hot lead?"

"Hot as blazes as it turned out."

She gave him an injured look. "That isn't funny."

"My grandma once told me that if you can laugh when they're pointing a pistol in your face then maybe you've got a sense of humor."

"How about when a good friend dies?"

"Then you have a real guffaw."

"You had quite a grandma, Radkin."

"You bet!"

He pulled over to the side of the road.

"Why are we stopping at this fast-food joint?" she asked.

"Listen to me, Kate," he said, "we don't have much to go on, but all roads seem to be leading to one place . . ."

She looked out the window. "Kentucky Fried Chicken?"

"No. To Hughes. I spoke to Mike's mother today. I forced the story about Singh out of her, but I think she wanted to tell me something else . . ."

"What?"

He ran his hand through his hair. "Well, I sort of blew it with her."

Her eyes grew big. "That's quite an admission."

"Yeah, I can take it. If I blow it, I blow it. And I blew it."

"So you want to try again?"

"It's not that easy. I think she's under surveillance."

"Why?"

He shrugged. "You got me."

She looked at him harshly. "You're not thinking of kidnapping anyone, are you?"

"What if I was?"

She thought a minute. "Just if it was the only way."

"I have another idea."

"What?"

"Sit in front of her house and wait for something to happen," he said, opening the door and getting out.

"So why are you getting out here?" she called through the window.

"If you're gonna have a stake out, you're gonna need provisions," he said, without looking back around.

The first rays of dawn bathed the tiny car in a halo of light. The neighborhood was still asleep when Joseph opened the door and got out for a stretch. He jogged down the street and grabbed a bottle of milk from the front door of a house that had a Tory sign. He took the newspaper too, and went back for a read and a drink.

He didn't see anything about Chancellor's body being found. But he wasn't sure it would make the press. What's an ex-cop's suicide compared to the important stories of the day, like the one that was headlined "Has Lovely Lisa's Lolly Popped?"

205

He used the morning rag to wrap up the discarded chicken bones and threw it down into the gutter.

At seven on the dot, the chauffeur drove a silver Rolls around to pick up Hughes.

"The big guy doesn't need much sleep," Joseph said to himself, jotting down a note.

A little after nine, Kate woke up. She stretched herself and straightened her hair. "Anything happen?" she asked.

"The master's left the lair," said Joseph, handing her a half-pint of cow juice.

She drank down the milk and stared up at the house. "What if she's not there?" Kate asked.

"Then we're out of luck," said Joseph, getting back in the car and sitting behind the wheel again.

Nothing of note happened till half-past ten when the butler who had strong-armed Joseph several days before came out and looked around. Joseph ducked down, sinking low into the seat. The butler took out a cigarette, had a smoke and then went down the drive toward the back of the house.

About fifteen minutes later, a tan Mercedes came down the inner drive.

"Hey, Radkin!" Kate jabbed him in the ribs.

"Cut it out!" he said, turning toward her. "It's the second time you did that!"

She pointed. Virginia Hughes had appeared at the door and was walking down the stairs.

"Hold onto your hat!" said Joseph, turning the ignition key. "This little jack rabbit's gonna catch itself a cat!"

They followed the Mercedes from the Hampstead digs straight into town.

"What if she's going to the dentist?" asked Kate.

"You're dealt a hand," he said, "you play it out."

"Radkin's theory of journalism or another quote from Grandma?"

"Grandma didn't play poker."

"Next left!" she said, pointing to the Mercedes which was three cars in front of them now.

He swung the Mini into the proper lane and, down-shifting, made the turn. "Hey, I kinda like this car!"

She made a face. "I think I know where she's heading. That's Knightsbridge over there."

"So where's she heading?" asked Joseph.

"Harrods, of course."

Kate was right. The Mercedes had stopped in front of the bustling store to leave Virginia Hughes off.

Joseph pulled the Mini over to the curb. As he did, a traffic warden came over to them and said, "You can't park here, sir. This is a restricted zone."

"Restricted for what?" asked Joseph, getting out from the Mini and joining Kate on the pavement.

"Deliveries."

"This is an Embassy car. I'm the American Ambassador and I was told that I could park wherever I liked," he said, taking Kate's arm and walking away.

"Excuse me, sir," she called after him. "You don't have diplomatic plates. Your car will be towed away!"

He turned toward her and shook his finger. "If you lay a hand on that car I'll have the entire American Air Force bomb Buckingham Palace!"

"You really know how to throw your weight around," said Kate, as they hurriedly made for Harrods.

"She won't dare touch it. You just have to exert a little authority with those kinds of people, that's all."

"Is that what your grandma taught you?" she asked. They pushed their way through the door. "She wasn't the American Ambassador, by any chance?"

"No, but she told me she once ate dinner at the Ambassador Hotel in New York."

The store was packed with fancy people trying to acquire even more trappings of wealth.

"I think we've lost her," said Kate. "She could be any-where."

"I have two suggestions," he said.

"What?"

"Jewels and furs."

She wasn't in jewels.

They found her in furs trying on a white mink coat.

"Listen," said Kate, as she and Joseph stood behind a rack of sable jumpers keeping watch. "Perhaps I should handle this."

Joseph rubbed his chin. "Maybe you're right."

He stayed where he was and Kate marched boldly over to Virginia Hughes. It was too far to hear. He saw it without words.

As Kate approached her, Virginia Hughes turned. Her face registered surprise. Kate said something. Virginia Hughes firmly shook her head, picking up her wrap as if making ready to go. Kate said something more forcefully. Virginia Hughes stopped in her tracks. Her faced tightened. Kate walked slowly over to where she was standing and gently put a hand on her shoulder. With a look of sadness, Virginia Hughes turned again. Kate said something else and Virginia Hughes nodded, took her wrap and left.

Kate came back to where Joseph was hidden behind the furs.

"What happened?" he asked. "Why'd you let her go?"

"She's meeting us in the tea-room," she said, taking him by the hand and pulling him along. "And Radkin . . ."

"Yeah?"

"Try very hard not to blow it again."

The service was silver this time. The napkins were cloth. The woman across from them was covered in furs and jewels and smelled like a bucket of flowers.

"I haven't much time," she said.

"If I had a bankroll like yours, lady, I'd have as much time as I want . . ." Joseph began.

208

Under the table, Kate gave him a kick as she reached out to touch the woman's hand. "Virginia, it's been a trying time for all of us."

The lady looked at Joseph. "My son respected you — heaven knows why."

"Maybe it's because I don't beat around the bush . . ." He caught himself this time. "Listen," he said, "I didn't know Mike that well but I did know his work and it was top notch. I know how much you have to put into it for it to come out like that."

"He was dedicated," said Virginia Hughes.

"We are too, Virginia," said Kate.

Virginia Hughes looked at Kate. Her face seemed to soften. "Would you have had his child?"

"I might have," she replied.

"But you were interested in your career . . ."

"He was interested in his career. I was interested in mine."

"Mrs Hughes, let me ask you something," said Joseph. "Was Ronald Chancellor brought to your house the night of the Palmerston hunt?"

Virginia Hughes turned to stare at him. "There's no getting round your directness, is there, Mr Radkin?" She sighed. "Mr Chancellor did come to the house, but as far as I can tell it was of his own volition."

Kate looked at her in surprise. "What did he want?"

"He wanted to meet with my husband, of course." Turning to Joseph, she said, "You're right about one thing, Mr Radkin. My husband is a detestable man."

"And detestable men do detestable things," said Joseph. "Is it possible that you overheard anything?"

"There is a room near my husband's office that I go to on occasion. I tend to spend more time there these days . . ."

"Tell us what you know, Virginia," said Kate. "Please . . ."

"Mr Chancellor came to the house, as I said. How the meeting was arranged, or why, I don't know. But Mr

209

Chancellor seemed to have some information that interested my husband very much."

"Was this the first time they met?"

"No. Mr Chancellor had visited my husband several times before."

"And this time he came to make a deal?" said Joseph.

"Perhaps. But people don't make deals with my husband, Mr Radkin. He makes deals with them."

"What did he want from your husband, then?" Joseph asked.

"I thought that would be obvious to a man like yourself," said Virginia Hughes.

"He wanted to get his daughter out of jail," said Kate.

"So what did Hughes suggest?" asked Joseph. "That he write a confession and stick a gun to his head?"

Virginia Hughes looked at him a moment and then said, "I don't know whether you're trying to be sarcastic, Mr Radkin, but in fact it was something like that, yes. My husband suggested to Mr Chancellor that it was the only way out for him. And that if he would also confess to the murder of my son, then my husband would see to it that Mr Chancellor's daughter would be freed from jail."

Kate closed her eyes. "So Ron killed Mike . . ."

Virginia Hughes reached over and touched her hand. "No. My husband was the one who killed my son."

"Do you have any evidence of that?" asked Joseph.

She shook her head. "But I know it to be the case. It wasn't my husband who did the act, of course. He wouldn't dirty his hands. Like most men in his position, he used a surrogate."

"But why?" asked Kate.

The muscles in the lady's face seemed to slacken as she said, "Because most of all he wanted what he couldn't have . . ."

She got up from her seat. She seemed to Joseph a sad and lonely figure now. "I must go," she said. "I can't be late. They get suspicious if I'm not on time."

"Mrs Hughes . . ." Joseph began. "What's the relationship between your husband and the Palmerstons?"

There was a slight smile on her face — a tired smile of irony. "He owns them, Mr Radkin. Didn't you know? Mr Chancellor did. My husband owns Foxton Manor . . ."

"And the stables?"

"He owns everything. They were in great distress some years ago. He bought their property — everything they own — and gave it back to them on lease."

"The horses as well?"

"Especially the horses, Mr Radkin. He loves to watch them run — and the knowledge he owns them, despite the fact that he does so in Palmerston's name, gives him an added thrill."

"Does he ever go up to the Newmarket races, Mrs Hughes?"

"As often as he can," she said. "Nearly every week."

"Did he ever meet Mike there?"

She looked at him and touched her own cheek gently with her hand. "I don't know it for a fact, Mr Radkin, but I suspect he met Michael at the Newmarket races the day of his death."

She started to walk away.

"Just one more thing, Mrs Hughes . . ." Joseph called after her.

She turned.

"Does your husband ever drive a black limousine with one-way glass? I saw it out in front of Chancellor's place yesterday."

"It belongs to his legal team, Mr Radkin. They probably went there to pick up the confession and to make sure the suicide was properly enacted."

Chapter 22

Of course the Mini had been towed away when they emerged from the fantasy world of Harrods.

"What did you expect?" she asked as they took the bus back to Gospel Oak.

"A little respect for your American cousins." Then, glancing at her sideways, he said, "What did you think of her?"

"Virginia? To be quite honest, I don't know what to make of her. Would I be trite if I said I'm left with a feeling of pity?" She looked down at her hands. "Do you think we've reached the end of the line, Radkin?"

"We might have," he said.

"I'd like to contact Lavinia's solicitor," said Kate. "If nothing else, at least we should be able to get the poor woman out of jail."

"OK," he said. "You try to call Bea Kendal. There are still a few things I have to take care of."

Upstairs, in his rooms, he poured himself some whisky from a bottle he had picked up on the way home. He fixed himself a drink, pulled out Mike's diary and went through it yet another time.

The entries for Mike's last day on earth were "H. T. — 10 a.m.". Then, "4th race — Newmarket." Meet H-g". In between, in a different color pen, was the notation "BM 6495aa56" and then the page number of a book.

The fourth race at Newmarket was late in the afternoon — Joseph had checked. Before Mike had gone there he had come back to his room and changed his shirt, leaving his diary behind. It took at least a couple of hours to get up to

Newmarket without a car. So if Mike had gone to the British Museum in between he must have been rushed.

Putting the diary aside, he worked out what time it would be in San Francisco and made a call.

The voice that answered was abrupt. "West here. What do you want?"

"Sorry for calling you at home," said Joseph. "But I figured you wake with the crow . . ."

"What's up, Radkin?"

"That great scoop Mike was so excited about — are you sure it had to do with the Maybrick case?"

"No. I just assumed it had to do with the assignment."

"What time was it when he phoned?"

"He called me at home — about the same time you're calling now."

"Can you remember exactly what he said?"

"I'm lucky if I remember my name at this hour. But the gist of it was that he had something boffo that he was going to send me that would make the earth shake. Mike used a lot of hyperbole though — even when he talked about a pair of shoes."

"But you never received it, did you?"

"He said he had some rough notes that he was working up. I guess it's with the missing stuff . . ."

"Maybe not," said Joseph. "I think I might know what he did with it."

"Listen," said West. "Find out what you can and then lay off. We can only invest so much in a fishing expedition. Besides, I got something urgent I want you to work on."

"Just another day or so," said Joseph.

"All right," said West. "Call me later at the office."

He took the bus to Bloomsbury again.

The woman at the library counter grimaced when she saw him.

"Remember me?" he said with a smile.

"You're the rhinocerus," she said. "How could I forget?"

"Still got my ticket," he said, flashing her the card. His picture had the same silly grin.

She closed her eyes. "Please. I haven't had my coffee yet."

"Got my book?"

"What book?"

"The one I asked for. You remember, had the number but no name . . ."

"Oh, that book. No, it's lost."

He looked at her for a minute, speechless for once in his life, and then, appearing truly crestfallen, silently turned around.

He was half-way out when she called to him: "Wait a minute."

He turned around again.

She motioned for him to come back.

"Here," she said, handing him an old volume. "Treat it with care."

He took the book. Looking at her curiously, he said, "Why did you do that?"

"I don't know," she said with a shrug. "It just seemed right somehow."

He took the book over to an empty table and sat down. He ran his hand over the cover and turned to the title page. The name of the book was *My Lost Fifteen Years*. The author was Florence Maybrick.

He quickly turned to page 101. There, tucked neatly into the spine, were several folded sheets of paper. He took them out and carefully unfolded them. He saw at once what it was. He scanned through and then, folding them again, put them in the pocket of his jacket.

Closing the book, he got up from his chair and was about to leave when he suddenly stopped and sat back down. He opened the book, turned to a page at random, and began to read.

It was Florence Maybrick's own story, simply told, of her life in prison after her death sentence was commuted.

He read it through. Then he closed the book. Several lines

ran through his mind. It was early on. Maybrick had written: "Once more I was led within the walls that were to be for years my tomb. Outside the sun was shining and the birds were singing."

He wrote it down. For, he thought, that was all that need be said.

Outside the British Museum he found a photocopy shop and made three copies of Mike's report. Afterwards, he purchased three manila envelopes, put one report in each, and addressed them.

He telephone Kate from a call box.

"I couldn't get hold of Bea Kendal," she said, "but her secretary said she was addressing a meeting of the Nuclear Waste Watchdog Committee at Friends Meeting Hall. If you hurry, you can just make it. I'd go myself but Sean is due back in an hour and I also have to pick up a little girl . . ."

"You Americans certainly do get around!" Beatrice Kendal said as Joseph hopped into her taxi.

"We have to if we want to keep up with people like you," he replied. He reached into his pocket and handed her the envelope with a copy of Mike's report. "Read this when you have a little time," he said. "It might give you some ammunition in your fight against the forces of evil."

"I appreciate your help, Mr Radkin," she said, opening up her tattered briefcase and slipping the envelope in. "But you could have sent this to me in the post. What was it that you wanted to see me about?"

"Did you hear about Ron Chancellor's suicide?"

She nodded her head. "I received notification this morning."

"I understand there was a confession."

"There was one sent to me by special messenger."

Joseph rubbed behind his ear. "What do you make of it?" he asked.

"You might ask what I make of confessions in general. At the best of times they're curious acts of atonement. But confessions discovered after death must always be suspect."

"So you don't believe it?"

"I neither believe nor disbelieve. I only doubt."

"Did you know Ron Chancellor was accused of poisoning his wife?"

"Ah," she said. "You wish to probe the mind of our departed friend . . ."

"He just didn't seem the type," Joseph said.

"Nor was he," Beatrice Kendal replied. "I don't know how you learned of this event in Mr Chancellor's past, but I wonder whether you also knew that his wife was inflicted with terminal cancer."

He shook his head. "I didn't."

"As a husband who was forced to watch his wife suffer through her last days of life, it's quite understandable that he would have been moved to help end her misery. As a policeman, of course, he was bound by the criminal code of law. The result was his resignation and, unfortunately, a tarnished record."

"Well," said Joseph, taking a cigarette and lighting up, "if nothing else, at least the unlucky bastard'll get his daughter out of jail."

"Ah," she said. "But there's the rub . . ."

He looked at her aghast. "You mean it won't?"

"The confession has no legal standing. Again, it was typed. There was no witness to his hand. But, most important, it could be claimed that as a father it was in his interest to exonerate his child."

Joseph inhaled deeply and let the smoke run from his lips. "So you're saying the poor kid will continue to rot in there."

"The wheels of justice move very slow, I'm afraid," she said, rolling down the window on her side of the cab.

On the way back to Gospel Oak he made a quick stop at the apartment house near Batty Street where Dr Singh had lived.

He knocked at the door of the woman he had spoken to the other day.

She looked at him through the crack in the chained door and said, "I told you all I know. Please go away."

"Just one thing more," he said. "Has someone else been around?"

"Yes," she replied.

"Tall and lean. Middle-aged. Face like a policeman?"

"Yes," she said, closing the door tight. "Please go away!"

Kate had just finished giving Sean a bath when he came in. She was downstairs rubbing him with a terry-cloth towel. Lavinia Chancellor's little girl was sitting across the room, staring at them with huge, expressionless eyes.

"She watches everything," said Kate, "but she never says a word."

"How come she's here?" asked Joseph.

"I phoned the woman who's fostering her. She let me take her for a visit."

Joseph looked over at the little girl. "She's got haunting eyes," he said. Turning to Kate, he continued, "She's lucky to have you for a friend."

"Lucky isn't how I'd describe her. Want some coffee?"

The kettle was already on the boil. She made a pot of filtered stuff and poured some into a mug for him.

He took one of the envelopes from his pocket and handed it to her.

"What's this?" she asked.

"Notes on Mike's interview with Singh — the researcher at Hughes Industries who filed a suit. It seems that Singh was looking into various possibilities for a new kind of stimulant, something that could keep the Yuppie workforce happy as they ran their treadmill far into the night. Anyway, he hit on something that really fit the bill. In proper doses it could make rats run mazes like they were on souped-up motor bikes. Not only could they continue without fatigue for hours, they actually seemed to increase their efficiency as time went on. And it had one other effect that really excited him . . ."

"Don't tell me it was also an aphrodisiac."

"You saw the film?" he asked with a certain amount of disappointment.

"I was being sarcastic."

"Well, it made the little critters as horny as hell. At least that's what Singh observed. So he wrote up his report and then a week later he's called in for a meeting with the big man himself . . ."

"You mean Cecil Hughes?"

"The one and only. Hughes is delighted. But to Singh's absolute horror, he wants to push it into production — fast! Which meant human experiments."

"Wait a minute," said Kate. "Why the hurry? Surely there are plenty of stimulants around."

Joseph shook his head. "We're talking about peak efficiency, Kate. There's big money in offering people that little edge. And if you can offer them sexual thrills as well, you've damn well made another fortune for yourself."

"Except for one thing . . ."

"Yeah," said Joseph. "Too much of it can kill you. Something that Singh pointed out. He cautioned against running human tests, but Hughes said it was necessary in order to probe the limits. He said it was one thing to run a rat through a maze, quite another to find out if humans could be kept at peak performance."

"So Singh relented?"

"For a while. The testing started — secretly, of course — and sure enough somebody died. Singh was overwhelmed with guilt and went to see Hughes at his Hampstead digs. That's when Mike's mother found out. And then she told Mike."

Kate looked down into the blackness of her coffee. "And Virginia is convinced that Hughes took his revenge." She looked up at Joseph again. "But she hasn't any proof, has she?"

218

Joseph shook his head. "Hughes didn't kill Mike, Kate," he said. "He wanted him killed, but he didn't pull the trigger."

"Who killed him then?" she asked.

"The same man who tried to kill me . . ."

He pulled out Mike's diary and turned to the final page. "Mike left this in his shirt pocket. Mrs White found it and gave it to me. It shows he had a meeting at ten a.m. the day he died. 'H. T.' stands for Hughes Towers. He went there after he had his interview with Singh."

"But then he went to Foxton Farms," said Kate.

Joseph shook his head again. "This says he went to Newmarket race-track. See?" He pointed to the scrawled notation. "'4th race—Newmarket. Meet H-g.' At first I thought that was Hughes. But the dash could be an 'o', don't you think?"

She glanced at it. Her face became sallow.

"Ron's middle name was Hogarth," said Joseph, looking at her determinedly.

She didn't meet his eye. "Mike used to call him that," she said.

"What?"

"He used to call him 'Hog'".

They sat quietly together in the kitchen while in the front room the two children were glued to the television set.

"I can't believe it," Kate said finally. "I trusted him so much . . ."

"He was the man caught in the middle, Kate. He made a pact with the devil and the devil won out."

"Virginia Hughes said he'd been to her house several times. How long do you think he was working for Hughes?"

Joseph shrugged. "I don't know. Probably sometime after he made the connection between Hughes and Palmerston — that Hughes owned the Palmerston estate. If Ron was actually trying to set Palmerston up in order to clear his daughter, he would have been feeding bits and pieces to Mike — like he tried to do with me. Ron knew that Fry was blackmailing Palmerston so he laid a trail to implicate him in order to clear his daughter's name. Ron probably thought he could go to Hughes with bargaining leverage — he knew Hughes was a man who could get things done. But Hughes would have found out pretty fast that Ron was desperate. And one thing's certain — Hughes has lots of experience dealing with desperate men."

"So he used Ron to go after Singh . . ."

"Yes. I confirmed that today. Mike must have put two and two together and confronted Ron with the facts."

"If that were so," said Kate, "why did he keep trying to implicate Palmerston after you came along? Why did he want to get you involved?"

"I was involved whether he wanted me involved or not. Anyway, he knew enough not to trust Hughes. Rightly or wrongly, he still felt the only way he could get his daughter free was by focusing attention on the hanging club and exposing Fry as a blackmailer. And he figured he could convince me there was a pattern of murders that lead directly to Palmerston. Of course, Hughes found out about it and laid a trap for him at the hunt."

"A trap?"

"Sure. He got Ron to try to kill me. But, really, he set him up."

"But what about Fry?" asked Kate. "Do you honestly think Ron killed him to save his daughter?"

Joseph didn't answer at first. Then he said, "I think we have to face the possibility that Lavinia actually killed her sadist lover."

Kate shook her head. "I'll never believe that!" she said. "You might as well say Maybrick killed her husband."

"Maybe she did," Joseph said. "But the point is that in neither case was it proven — not to my satisfaction. Both of them were victims in the end."

She poured him another cup of coffee. "No easy solutions, are there?" she said.

"Not in life. But there are greater and lesser degrees of guilt."

"And I know a greater one whose goose I'd like to cook!" she said.

Joseph nodded. "So do I."

He phoned West from his room.

"You got your story?" West asked him.

"It might cause some heat when I write it up."

"Let's take a look at it," said West. "If it's good we'll publish it."

"You'll be putting your magazine at risk," said Joseph. "These people know their stuff."

"OK," said West, "fair warning. Where are you now?"

"Mike's room."

"Time to pull the plug," he said. "I've got a new assignment for you."

"I'd like to stick with this one a bit longer."

"Maybe sometime you can do a follow-up . . ."

He packed up his stuff. He left everything the way it had been, except for the banana cup which he took as a memento. He wrote a note and left some money for Mrs White.

Leaving the house, he walked across the street and went up to her door. He stood there for a moment. Inside he heard voices. A mother talking to her son. He waited, looked down at the scuff marks on his shoe. And then he left.

He grabbed a cab at South End Green.

"Where to?" asked the driver.

"Heathrow," he said. "But drive through the center of town."

"It's longer that way," the cabby said.

"So what?" said Joseph.

They drove a while and when they reached the river Joseph said, "Stop here. I'm getting out."

He paid the cabby and walked along the Embankment. He found a phone box and made a call.

221

"Hi," he said when she answered. "I wanted to say goodbye . . ."

"I suspected that," she said.

"Not forever."

"Not forever's still a long time."

"It's an important story, but it'll be hard as hell to follow up. You gonna do it?"

"I might," she said. "There's still an innocent woman in jail and a rat bastard who thinks he's won. Someone's got to do it."

"I've got a friend I think you should call. His name's McIssacs. He'd like to help. Maybe I'll give him your number, OK?"

"Don't do me any favors, Radkin."

"You're all right, Kate. You're a damn fine journalist."

"Have you ever read my stuff?"

"No."

"So how do you know?"

"I know, OK?"

"Listen, I have to go now, Radkin. Feeding time for the kid. You know how that is . . ."

"Yeah. See you around."

"Sure. See you around, Yank. Give me a call next time you're in town." And she hung up.

Near to where he stopped to make the call was a liquor shop. He went inside and looked around. Then he went up to the proprietor and pointed to a box.

"You want that?" asked the proprietor, dusting it off. "The entire case?"

"Yes," said Joseph. "If you can deliver it to Kilburn."

"Deliver it?" said the proprietor. "It's been sitting here for years! If you buy it, I'll hump it to China myself for you. Nobody drinks grappa anymore!"

"There's a message that goes with it," said Joseph, taking out the envelope containing the third copy of Mike's notes. He took a clean piece of paper and wrote: "McIssacs —

222

thanks for your help. Here's something you can follow up. PS: There's a dynamite journalist named Kate O'Malley who cooks cannelloni like you've never dreamed. She's been in on the story and she's expecting your call. She can be pissy at times, so don't let her put you off." He wrote in the number and signed his name.

He continued walking east till he reached the City. In the forest of concrete towers he came to one that he knew well. Across the street, sitting in its shadow, was a small sausage-and-beans café. He went inside, found a table and sat down.

An elderly waitress came over to him. "What'll you have, luv?"

"A cup of tea," he said. "For old time's sake, OK?"

"Coming up."

She brought it over, milky brown.

"Nice to see a place like this still around," he said.

"Not for long," she replied. "Next year we'll be torn down."

"That building over there," said Joseph, pointing in the direction of the looming shadow. "You know it?"

"Hughes Towers?" she said. "They've bought this entire row. Going to build the world's biggest bank."

"World's biggest, huh?"

"I've been here fifty years," she said. "Never missed a day's work." She sighed. "That's all over now. But it's been a good life, can't complain . . ."

"Did you try — complaining, that is?"

She laughed. "Blimey! We're just a little café!"

He watched the waitress walk slowly back to her post behind the counter and then he opened his suitcase and took out his writing stuff.

He started his article. This is how it began:

"Almost fifty years ago, around the time America joined Britain in the Great War to protect democracy and human rights, there was a death in a small New

223

England town. An old woman was found rotting in a shack. When they discovered her body, several days after her death, the place was a mess. Open cans of mouldering food were littered on the floor, old copies of the *New York Times* lay in a heap and everything was covered with the feces of cats. In fact, cats were everywhere. Hundreds of them. People said later they were her only friends. Cats and dogs and birds — any creature of the wild.

"The woman's name was Florence Maybrick. And few, if any, people in that small New England town knew that fifty years before she had been in a Liverpool jail, watching from a window in her stone-cold cell her gallows being built.

"So what does this unhappy woman who died alone in an American village so far from her Victorian prison have to do with a mad judge, a hanging club, a Jewish umbrella-stick maker, a dead ex-cop and a little girl with haunting eyes whose mother is now languishing in jail in London, England? And what does any of this have to do with a chemist who once worked for Hughes Industries and is now in hiding for his life in his native India?

"Well, read on folks! 'Cause these questions and more provide the subject for this month's spine-tingling investigation by yours truly, Joseph Radkin . . ."